# MODEEN CONVERGENCE

## FRANK H JORDAN

The situations, organisations, and characters in this book are fictional, and any resemblance to an existing or past entity is entirely coincidental.

**This book is written in Australian English.**

*To my co-author, best friend, and wife. Thanks for all your hard work and inspiration. Without your support these books may never have been.*

# THE MISSION

## Provide additional security detail

For the premier's planned visit to Cairns in far north
Queensland, the Feds call on national security agency
NatSec to provide assistance with the protection detail.
Agent Jo Modeen is assigned the task, what she
considers to be a 'babysitting' job ... that is, until an
attempt is made on her own life.
Modeen's old unit converges to take on what becomes
a complex mission.
One with dangerous links to the past....

# CHAPTER ONE

ASIO agent John Dylan pulled into the Rous Head carpark at Port Fremantle in Western Australia. Under the cloudless sky of a perfect summer morning passengers bustled about, dropping off luggage and jostling for positions on the jetty.

From the rear of the carpark, Dylan sank low in the seat of his government-issue sedan and eyed his target through binoculars while pressing his mobile against the side of his face. Lowering the binoculars, he ran a hand over his receding hairline.

*Hurry up and wait ... that's what this job's all about.*

He heaved a sigh as his call was answered. Putting the binoculars to his eyes again he barked, 'Dylan, reporting in. Washington has purchased a ticket and appears to be taking the nine-thirty ferry to Rotto.' After listening for a few moments, he clicked off the phone and slipped it back into his shirt pocket.

Donning dark sunglasses and pulling a cap down over his eyes, he got out of the car to stroll nonchalantly across the carpark to the ticket counter, where he joined the queue. When it was his turn to be served, he tipped his cap at the large woman seated behind the counter. 'Ticket for the next ferry, thanks love. Oh, and a copy of today's paper.'

The woman took a hasty sip from her paper cup. Wishing the customers would stop coming so she could take a proper break, she pulled a face at the coffee's luke-warm temperature and eyed the tall, solidly-built man smiling across the counter at her. Dressed in blue denim jeans and floral Hawaiian shirt, he looked like every other ferry traveller. But when she glanced down to check for carry-on luggage, his black business shoes caught her eye. Most people taking the ferry wore holiday-type footwear – sandals, thongs or even bare feet. With a mental shrug and thinking *each to his own,* she put down her cup, took his proffered money and handed him a ticket and the newspaper.

Nodding his thanks, he moved to the far end of the boarding area and took a seat away from the other waiting passengers. Shaking open the newspaper, he lifted his gaze to just above the pages and scanned for his target, locating the fit-looking, twenty-something African-American loitering by the jetty fence. As he watched, the man ran a large hand over his military-styled buzz cut before bending to lean both arms on the top railing and stare out to sea.

When the boarding call squawked from the speakers mounted around the waiting area, Dylan lowered the newspaper and watched his target join the queue preparing to board the scrubbed and gleaming *Egret Express* bobbing gently beside the jetty.

As he rose to join the queue himself, Dylan heard his target exchanging pleasantries with the crew like he was a regular commuter to the island.

'Hey Eli, you're in for a treat this morning,' one of the crew members called from where he was busy loading luggage in the hold. 'There's a Yankee aircraft carrier moored just outside the heads.'

'I know,' Washington called back in a noticeably American accent. 'She's the *Carl Vinson,* a Nimitz-class aircraft carrier.'

'Oh yeah?'

'Yeah, she arrived last night after six months in the Arabian Gulf. Will be heading back to San Diego next week.'

'You sure know your shit, man.' The crew member threw him a grin before hurrying astern in response to the captain's insistent gesturing.

From where he stood back in the queue, John Dylan watched his target wave a nonchalant hand at the crew member before making his way up the inner stairs. The man moved with ease, the long limbs of his dark-skinned body working smoothly together like a well-oiled, muscular machine. Taking his usual seat on the top deck, he leaned back in the chair, kicked off his thongs, and rested his feet on the deck railing.


The *Egret Express* gave the *Carl Vinson* a wide berth as they passed, while passengers on both decks of the ferry craned their necks to get a better view of the aircraft carrier.

From his perch on the top deck, Eli Washington slouched in his seat, shaded his eyes and squinted at the carrier until it was left behind in the ferry's frothy wake. Powering through the channel at twenty-eight knots, the *Egret Express* arrived at the island half an hour later, where it docked smoothly at its usual mooring in Thomson Bay.

Amid the rush of crew members tying up the ferry and preparing to unload holiday makers, luggage, bicycles and provisions onto the small jetty, Washington made his way down the stairs and off the ramp.

He strolled down the jetty, whistling, and took the first road to the left, taking care to dodge a family of tourists wobbling down the road on hired pushbikes.

Feeling his phone vibrate with an incoming call, he took it from the side pocket of his cargo pants, tapped on the screen and put it to his ear.

'You're being followed,' a female voice purred.

Washington's broad lips tipped into a smug grin. His pace didn't slow as he drawled, 'Tall guy, red Hawaiian shirt, cap and dark sunnies?'

'Yes.'

'Should I take him on a tour?'

'No, lead him back to base.' The voice paused. 'Looks like our cover's blown. Time to move camp again.'

'Damn! I liked it here.' Washington scowled. 'He's gonna pay for makin' me leave.' Tapping his phone to end the call, he took up whistling again as the road led him southward. At the Kingstown Barracks turn-off, he left the bitumen and made his way to the front of the compound.

The austere red-brick barracks complex, built in the 1930s to accommodate the thousands of troops stationed on the island in WW2, was dominated by a clock tower that overlooked the parade ground. A salvaged six inch BL Mk XI gun barrel from Bickley Battery had been mounted in pride of place at the entrance to the ground.

Adjacent to the barracks, a cluster of buildings that had housed the officers' mess, canteen, married quarters, and offices of the Royal Australian Artillery and Royal Australian Engineers, sat empty and silent.

After the army handed the site over to the state government in the 1980s, the barracks had been partly refurbished for use as holiday accommodation. But when the restoration work ground to a halt after funding ran out, the accommodation option was reduced to special occasion bookings only. Being situated away from the main shopping and entertainment precinct meant visits to Kingstown were limited to the occasional camera-toting, cycling tourist. But as the sun's heat intensified during the day even the most avid tourist sought cooler activities, leaving the site eerily deserted by all but the ghosts of the past.

Stopping on the side of the road a hundred metres back from the barracks, John Dylan pulled out his phone and was about to put it to his ear when a female voice hissed, 'I'll take that.'

He felt a sharp poke in the back and froze. Turning his head slowly to look over his shoulder, he saw a shapely olive-skinned woman standing behind him.

'Hand it over.' She prodded him again, between the shoulder blades this time so he could see the nine millimetre jet black Glock she was holding. Her grasp on the gun was easy, familiar. Here was someone well acquainted with its use.

He passed his phone to her without speaking and raised his hands in surrender.

Knocking his arms back down, she hissed, 'Keep 'em down, and don't attract any attention or it'll be the last thing you do.' With a quick scan to left and right, and finding the road behind and ahead of them clear of all but a few mildly inquisitive quokkas, she dropped his phone to the bitumen and stomped it with the heel of her boot.

'Now start walking.' Seeing Dylan wince at the sound of shattering and glance down at the innards of his mobile – his only means of communication – lying crushed on the bitumen like mechanical viscera, she smirked and gave him another sharp prod with the pistol. 'Move.'

Washington strode through the main hall behind the clock tower, his footsteps echoing on the wooden floor boards.

Polished to a dull shine by the purposeful tread of numerous army boots over the years – marching, snapping to attention, occasionally dancing – the boards were now covered in a gritty layer of sand and dust.

As he made his way through the spacious room, the old air stirred and the faded Army curtains still hanging in the windows twitched, only to fall back into morose stillness when he exited to the barracks' rear wing.

On reaching the six foot high security fence, erected during the restoration work to restrict access by the public, he met the woman by the chained and padlocked side security gate. She stood with one hand on Dylan's arm and the other pressing the muzzle of the Glock against his neck.

Throwing the woman a half-smart smirk, Washington pushed the gates apart and squeezed through the gap allowed by the slack in the chain. The woman rolled her eyes at him while shoving Dylan forward.

They followed Washington through a set of solid double doors and into the empty structure. Its interior had been gutted. New plasterboard covered most of the walls, but the ceiling joists lay bare.

Their footsteps echoed hollowly on the jarrah floor as they passed empty rooms before stopping at a small storage alcove at the end of the corridor.

Going to the back wall, Washington lifted the lump of two-by-four hardwood resting there and used it to tap three times on the floor. The sound of timber against timber still reverberated in the room when a metallic clunk came in reply.

Kneeling, Washington pulled open a trap door and gestured with his hand while giving their prisoner a smarmy smile. 'Down you go.'

Dylan hesitated and glanced sideways at his female captor. This earned him another sharp prod, this time in the back of the neck, and a snarled, 'Move.'

He stumbled forward and then gathered himself to descend a set of concrete steps. These led to a subterranean bunker that spanned the full length of the building. A solitary table and chair sat in the middle of the room, illuminated by a single light bulb suspended directly above. The rest of the cavern was shrouded in darkness, the only sound the rasp of human breathing.

'SIT DOWN.' The man's command rumbled from the inky blackness of the far corner.

The woman pushed Dylan into the chair, as she and Washington took positions on either side of him. Taking a plastic wire tie from the table, Washington reefed Dylan's wrists behind his back and bound them.

'Who are you, and why are you following us?' The man's voice once more echoed out of the darkness.

'My name's John Dylan. I'm a field officer with the Australian Security Intelligence Organisation. I had orders to check out a lead.'

'What lead?'

'Look, I'm unarmed, and as far as I know you guys aren't wanted for anything. I'm a federal officer, but if you let me go I won't press charges.'

Pulling a ten inch bowie knife from a scabbard hanging on the wall behind them, Washington leaned in to press the blade against Dylan's throat.

'What do you know about us?' the voice snarled.

'I have no idea who this woman is,' Dylan replied, lifting his chin to the right and then sucking in a breath and stiffening when the knife blade tightened against his neck. 'But old mate on my left here goes by the name Eli Washington. And I'm guessing you're Kyle Davidson ... although they aren't your real names, are they?'

'What *are* our real names?' The voice resonated with quiet menace.

'I don't know, and right now, I don't care.' Feeling added pressure against his throat and the sting of the blade as it broke through the first layer of skin, Dylan grimaced and said in a strangled voice, 'A-All I know is that you're s-supposed to be dead.'

At that, the man emerged from the dark corner and walked toward the chair, where he stood staring down into Dylan's face, his expression tight. 'Let's keep it that way.'

Dylan blinked back at him, eyes widening as he was struck with a bleak realisation and a sudden onset of gut-wrenching fear.

A thin trail of blood oozed from beneath the blade's edge at his throat, and mounting terror emanated from his every pore. The man staring down at him gave a derisive sniff, and then turned to nod curtly at Washington before once more melting into the darkness.

———

Luke Jackson dropped the dumbbell and picked up his NatSec phone. Placing it to his ear, he puffed, 'Williams.'

'It's Ben, Spook.'

'Hey Ben.'

'I need you to follow up on an ASIO agent who went missing twenty-four hours ago. I've cleared it with your team leader. You're to be at Garden Island naval base by twenty-one hundred.'

'I'll be there. So what's the go?'

'The agent's name is John Dylan and his last known position puts him just outside of Kingstown Barracks on Rottnest Island. A patrol boat, the HMAS Albany, will take you to the island, and four clearance divers will assist you. They're members of a tactical assault team that operates out of the naval base. I'll send you the details and a schematic of the barracks.' Ben paused. 'Dylan was following up a lead on two missing persons and could've met with foul play. So watch your six.'

'Always do.' The call ended and Spooky checked the time on his phone.

*Nineteen ten.*

From his apartment in Fremantle it would take roughly an hour to get to Garden Island naval base. Putting away his gym gear, he nipped into the bathroom for a quick shower and then packed his duffel and made his way to the basement.

Unlocking the boot of his black Toyota Aurion, he lifted the floor cover and transferred a Glock17, MP5SD6 assault rifle, and ammo into his bag. Throwing the duffel onto the back seat, he jumped behind the wheel and set off southward on Marine Terrace. His phone chimed with an incoming message and he glanced at the screen.

*Event 0739 – 4 attachments.*

Focusing his attention on the road ahead, he left the highway and made his way through Rockingham and on to Point Peron. A dual lane bridge spanned the five kilometres connecting the Royal Australian Naval Base to the mainland. Turning right onto the Garden Island causeway he was stopped at the main checkpoint. It was brightly illuminated and stood out like a beacon in the gathering darkness.

The guard eyed Spooky's NatSec ID which displayed his operational alias, and then leaned down to peer into his face before announcing, 'They're expecting you, Mr Williams.' He pointed down the road. 'Keep to the causeway. About six clicks down, turn right at the first barracks you come to.' He straightened. 'Welcome to the HMAS Stirling naval base. Have a good night, sir.'

'Thanks.' Giving the guard a lazy salute, Spooky eased the car away and cruised down the causeway, which ran straight as a die for three kilometres before veering slightly left. The road was flanked on both sides by the Indian Ocean, and Spooky found the moon's light reflecting off the rippling water mesmerising. He was abruptly snapped out of the trance when the car bumped as the bitumen spilled out onto the island.

Thinking, *not a bad night for a cruise*, he turned right at the first barracks. The car's headlights illuminated a Hawkei 4WD vehicle parked beside the barracks, with four naval seaman dressed in camouflage gear leaning against it. When Spooky pulled up beside the vehicle, one of the seamen waved him over.

'Jump in, mate.'

Glimpsing an emblem on the man's right shoulder, a crown on top of a diving helmet with a bold capital C beneath it, Spooky recognised it as a Senior Clearance Diver's badge. He grinned. 'We're not going to be doing much diving, you realise?' Getting out of the Aurion, he reached into the back seat and hauled out his duffel, slinging it over a compact but muscular shoulder.

'Huh,' the Lieutenant grunted. 'We don't just *dive*.' At Spooky's amused snort, he went on. 'I'm Anton Hessler, and this is my team; Chief Petty Officers Mansel Cummings, Ralph Dargaville, and Leading Seaman Mike Ellis.'

Spooky studied Anton's face while shaking his hand. 'We've met before … Afghanistan wasn't it?'

It was Anton's turn to peer at the newcomer, and after a second his frown turned into a grin. 'That's right, at the Multi-National Base at Tarin Kowt, in Urozgan. You were in Ben Logan's unit if I remember rightly, and were just bugging out as I arrived.'

Spooky nodded. 'Right,' and clapped his hands together. 'Okay, let's get this show on the road.' He threw his duffel into the back of the Hawkei and all five climbed aboard.

Anton drove around the barracks and pulled up at pier one, alongside the fifty-seven metre long *HMAS Albany,* an Armidale class patrol boat. Standing at anchor on its port side, the hundred and eighteen metre *HMAS Toowoomba* frigate dwarfed the patrol boat. On the Hawkei's arrival, the *Albany's* twin V-sixteen diesel motors fired up, and as soon as the five were on board it motored out of Careening Bay.

Anton gathered them in a small briefing room in the forward hull, and spread a map of Rottnest Island on the meeting table. The other four team members moved in close as he tapped a finger on the map.

'The *Albany* will drop us off here, on the lea side of

Twin Rocks, approximately two hundred and fifty metres from the island. We'll take a Zodiac and beach here,' and he tapped another spot on the map, 'at Bickley Bay.' He looked up at Spooky. 'Of course you'll be in charge of operations, Mr Williams. I believe our target is Kingstown Barracks?'

'Correct.' Spooky glanced up at the fifty-two inch monitor attached to the wall of the bulkhead and took a moment to sync his phone to it via Bluetooth. Bringing up the picture Ben had sent him of John Dylan, he went on. 'We're looking for this missing ASIO agent. He's been out of communication for the last twenty-four hours, and his last known location was just outside the barracks.'

He tapped on his phone and a schematic of the barracks appeared on the screen. 'We need to sweep the complex and surrounding area, under cover. As you know, this is a holiday destination and we're likely to encounter some wayward civilians even at this hour of the night. So stealth at all times, people.'

He pointed to a spot on the map just above the barracks. 'Cummings, I want you to cover the north. Dargaville east, and Ellis the west side of the barracks. When you're in position, Anton and I will move in from the south. The separate wing at the rear of the main building is under repairs and has been fenced off from the public.'

He turned back to the monitor and zoomed in on the rear barracks. 'Our schematic shows a bunker running under the entire length of this wing. If our man's being held captive, this would be a likely spot for them to stash him.'

Cummings spoke up. 'Captive by whom?'

Spooky glanced at him. 'Unknown. He was following up a lead on two missing persons and could've met with foul play, so we may encounter hostiles.' He swept a glance over the group. 'Any other questions?' When they shook their heads, he straightened. 'OK, let's suit-up.' Unzipping his duffel he pulled out the MP5, removed the magazine, checked the breech and placed the rifle on top of the table.

'You heard the man,' Anton barked. 'Let's move.'

# CHAPTER TWO

The *HMAS Albany's* radar, GPS and other instrumentation cast an eerie green glow around the bridge and over the captain, standing silently at the controls.

As he throttled back on the approach to Twin Rocks, the rumble of the motors dwindled to a low hum.

At the rear of the boat Spooky and the assault team climbed into the Zodiac, a seven metre, rigid-hulled inflatable, cradled on the starboard deck. Anton distributed comms units and then nodded to the crewman at the davit controls.

As the *Albany* slowed to a stop the Zodiac was lifted off the deck and lowered smoothly into the water.

In position at the centre console, Anton fired up the three hundred horsepower Yanmar diesel engine and eased the Zodiac's controls forward. The craft responded instantly, lifting its bow as a rooster-tail of white water gushed from its rear jet. Assisted by the on-board DGPS and radar, Anton snaked the inflatable around Twin Rocks, skilfully navigating between an expanse of limestone reef and into Bickley Bay.

The crew fitted their night vision goggles and braced themselves as the boat surged up onto the sand. Anton cut the motor and hastened to secure the anchor, while Spooky led the rest of the team up the beach and into the thick heath bushes of the sand dunes.

Keeping low, they followed a narrow sandy trail to the top of a ridge overlooking Kingstown Barracks, where a solitary floodlight cast a faint glow across the parade ground in front of the main building. There was no sign of movement anywhere, the place appeared deserted.

Spooky pointed a finger at Ellis and indicated the western side of the boundary, then waved Dargaville and Cummings to the east. Without a sound they peeled off and circled round to take up position.

Anton met Spooky at the top of the ridge and checked his watch.

*Twenty-two thirty.*

The team sounded off over the comms, their voices harsh whispers.

'Cummings in position.'

'Dargaville in position.'

'Ellis ready.'

Slinging their rifles across their backs, Spooky and

Anton crawled on their stomachs and then slid down the sandy trail toward the rear of the barracks. When they reached the security fence, Spooky took a quick scan of the metal mesh and then pulled a small pair of bolt cutters from out of his vest. He wasted no time cutting a single strand and unravelling it from the mesh to make a large enough hole for them to slip through. Clearing the fence, they braced their backs against the side of the building and took a moment to check for noise or movement.

Nothing.

Spooky bent low and led the way to the front of the main wing, followed closely by Anton. When they reached the entrance he raised a halting hand and then inched forward to test the solid double doors. Feeling movement at his tentative tug, he paused, realising they were unlocked.

Carefully opening one side of the door a crack, he leaned back holding his arm at full stretch. Half expecting a booby-trap, he used the barrel of his rifle to thrust the door open. It gave a silence-shattering creak as it swung on its hinges and he froze, holding his breath. But there was no explosion, no responding sound at all, and no sign of movement anywhere.

Inside the building the silence was thick, almost palpable, and the air held an ominous stench, one he had smelled too often before. Anton moved up to cover him as he hastened through the doorway, and then followed him inside. Through their night vision goggles the new plasterboard walls were a bright green haze, in contrast to the galvanised sheets and exposed joists of the inner roof.

The two men moved silently in unison as they passed empty rooms down each side of the hallway, and came to a stop at a small storage alcove. Pointing the muzzle of his rifle at a trap door latch, Anton made to move toward it when Spooky pulled him back. Holding up a hand and giving a vigorous shake of his head, Spooky disappeared down the hallway to return seconds later carrying a ball of carpenter's string wrapped around a piece of scrap wood.

After unwinding a good five metres from it, he tied the end of the string to the trap door latch and then threw the remaining roll over one of the ceiling joists. Bending to collect it again, he indicated to Anton to follow him and made his way to the far side of the alcove, where they both hunkered down behind a storage partition.

Pulling the string, Spooky took up the slack and the trap door slowly began to lift.

It wasn't until the door was half open that it exploded off its hinges, shattering the silence. The men ducked as splintered wood ricocheted around them and a plume of dust engulfed the alcove.

'Lieutenant?' The anxious voices of Dargaville, Ellis and Cummings broke comms silence.

Anton couldn't speak at first over the dust in his throat.

'*Lieutenant?*' Dargaville's voice was more urgent.

Anton coughed, spat and barked hoarsely, 'Hold your positions.'

Spooky waited for the dust to settle before creeping forward to the trap door opening where he lay flat on his stomach. Keeping a firm grip on his night vision goggles, he hung his head over the edge and peered into the void.

Rising to his feet, he waved Anton over, before climbing down the cement stairs into the bunker. After first checking they were still alone, Anton followed Spooky down and found him standing over a man's body seated at a table in the centre of the room. The man's hands were bound behind his back and he'd slumped forward onto the table. His face rested in a pool of congealed blood – his own, judging by his wounds – which had also soaked into his collar and stained the front of his Hawaiian shirt.

Anton stared down at the bloodied corpse and frowned. 'The agent?'

Spooky nodded and put a hand on the dead man's back. 'Rigor mortis has well and truly set in.' Grimacing, he withdrew his hand. 'Judging by that and the smell, my guess is he's been dead for well over twelve hours.'

'Do we take him back to the Zodiac? We've got a body bag on board.'

'No.' Spooky stepped away from the table and turned to Anton. 'Ben'll want to send in a forensic team. I'll call it in, and meet you back at the Zodiac.' As he spoke, he pulled his mobile from the side pocket of his black cargo pants.

Nodding, Anton pressed a finger to his comms piece. 'Rendezvous back at the Zodiac. Whatever went down here, we've missed it.' He turned and disappeared up the stairs.

Spooky tapped a number on the screen and put the mobile to his ear. After the first ring, he heard Ben bark, 'Report.'

'We found Dylan. He was still in the bunker, bound and with his throat slit.' Spooky waited, but the only sound from the other end of the line was a heavy sigh. He imagined Ben shaking his bent head. 'There're no visible signs of bruising,' he went on, 'or any indication he'd been tortured in any way.'

'How long has he been dead?' Ben's voice was flat, unemotional.

'Twelve hours at least, and the bunker's been stripped clean.' Spooky paused. 'Poor bastard was unarmed … didn't stand a chance. When is ASIO going to allow their agents to carry weapons?'

'May not have made any difference,' Ben said solemnly. 'This was only supposed to be a surveillance mission. He shouldn't have made contact under any circumstances.' He sighed again. 'I've got a clean-up team and chopper on stand-by. They'll be there within the hour.'

'Right. Well, there's nothing more I can do here. The

perps are long gone now, I'd reckon. But I'll check for tracks outside the barracks before I bug out with the tactical team.'

'I want you back on the island in the morning. I've been in contact with Dylan's operations manager and he confirmed the ID of one of the suspects. I'll send you some photos to flash around. See if you can get a positive ID on his accomplice, and dig up any info you can get on them.'

'Roger.' Spooky tapped End Call and made his way back up the bunker's concrete steps.

The tactical team was huddled around the front of the Zodiac peering into the sand dunes when, from out of the gloom, Spooky sidled up behind them. Sensing a presence at his side, Anton gasped and whirled around.

'What the— Where did you come from?'

Spooky grinned and then sobered. 'I followed their tracks across to Thomson Bay on the eastern side of the island. It looks like they left by boat.'

Anton frowned. 'You tracked them in the dark?'

'It's not that difficult in the sand dunes. Judging by the tracks there were three insurgents, two of fairly heavy build and one smaller or lighter weight.'

With a bemused shake of his head, Anton turned to put both hands on the front of the Zodiac. 'Let's get back to the Albany.'

The others joined him in pushing the boat off the beach and into the dark, still water of Bickley Bay. Once back on board, they removed their night vision goggles as Anton took up the controls at the centre console.

He turned to Spooky. 'By the way, how'd you know that trap door was wired?'

Throwing him a grin, Spooky said, 'Let's just say Modeen's radar has rubbed off on me.'

Anton gave a puzzled frown. 'Modeen's radar?'

Spooky patted him on the back. 'Another story for another time, my friend.'

# CHAPTER THREE

J osephine Modeen sat on the edge of her bed, head bent, intent on her task. She'd thrown a thick cotton blanket over her pretty doona to protect it while she field-stripped her Walther PPQ nine millimetre pistol. From the chamber end, she inserted a brush into the bore of the barrel and pushed it through until the bristles exited at the breech.

The shrill chime of the doorbell disturbed the industrious quiet and broke her concentration. She glanced at the digital clock on the dresser. It read *15:00* on the screen.

*Damn! Aunty Hann's early.*

Swiftly re-assembling the weapon, she returned it to its custom aluminium carrying case. It sat snuggly in a cut-away, just below the barrel and detached trigger assembly of a Vanquish sniper rifle. Snapping the lid closed, she spun the lock tumblers and placed the case in a corner of the bedroom. Plucking the blanket from off the bed, she dropped it over the case as she made her way out of the room. Hurrying to the front door, she checked the peep hole out of habit before unlocking and opening the door.

'Hello love.' Hannah Bourne stood outside the entrance with a small suitcase in each hand, appearing a little flustered. She gave a wry smile. 'It took a few tries but I managed to punch in the building key code you sent me.' Dropping the cases by her sides, she stepped forward to give Modeen a warm hug. 'You're looking lovely, dear.' Holding her niece at arms length she gave her firm biceps a squeeze. 'Still working out, I see.'

Modeen beamed at her. 'Hey Aunty Hann, it's lovely to see you,' adding with a fond shake of her head, 'come on in.'

She bent to collect the cases as her aunt bustled into the apartment.

'Thanks for letting me stay on such short notice. This seminar must be going to be huge, it seems every accommodation place within cooee is sold out.'

Modeen grinned to herself, thinking that was probably more to do with the Pink concert happening the same weekend.

Glancing around at the stylish penthouse, Hannah gave an appreciative nod at the neat minimalism, with occasional touches of feminine personality. Then her eyes fell on a stack of rifle range targets lying on the counter, all with bullet holes tightly clustered around the centres.

She paused to throw Modeen a significant glance. 'I know you can't talk about what you do in the armed forces, but you're keeping yourself safe, aren't you? Not taking too many risks?'

'Don't worry, not only am I careful, but my team mates won't let anything bad happen to me.' When Troy Wolverton's face sprang to mind, Modeen turned away in case her expression revealed more than she wanted her keen-eyed aunt to see.

Gathering up the targets, she bundled them into the bin. 'And it's no trouble having you here, Aunty Hann. Although I wasn't expecting you 'til a bit later.' She turned back with a smile. 'Like I said, I'll be away for a few days anyway so you'll have the place to yourself. And it's an easy walk from here to your seminar at the convention centre.'

'Excellent.' Hannah pondered her for a moment before speaking again. 'And good to know you're looking after yourself.' Brightening, she gushed, 'It's not every day I get a chance to stay in a penthouse on the Gold Coast!' She swept another glance around the apartment, noting the absence of masculine presence. 'Still live here by yourself, love?'

'Yep.'

Hannah shook her head. 'A gorgeous girl like you … it always surprises me that you haven't been snapped up, pronto.'

Modeen kept her expression neutral. 'Plenty of time for that, Aunty Hann. Now, let's get you settled.' Smiling fondly at her aunt, she led the way down the hall to the spacious guest room.

Hannah followed her into the room eyeing the gleaming off-white floor tiles, crisp blue and white coverlet on the queen-sized bed, and the floor-to-ceiling windows. Their white plantation shutters were open, revealing views over Surfers Paradise's main beach and the Pacific Ocean.

Going to stand by the windows, she breathed, 'Ooh, very nice, dear. I can see why you let your parents convince you to stay here.'

Modeen raised a rueful eyebrow. 'I didn't have much choice in the matter, they made me owner on the title … but it is a nice place to live, and I'm glad you like it.'

'I do, very much.' Hannah turned with a grin. 'Although it's a shame such a nice place came with a broken kettle.' She threw her niece a wink.

Modeen laughed. 'It was working fine this morning, and I'll make sure it still is while you get settled.' Leaving her aunt to unpack, she made her way into the kitchen.

Filling the kettle, she set it to boil while taking out two fine china cups from the deep crockery drawer and setting them on the gold-flecked white granite bench top.

'White tea with one, Aunty Hann?' she called.

'Thanks love,' came the response from down the hall. 'Be there in a sec.'

Modeen had just finished adding milk to their drinks when Hannah joined her.

'Woooh,' she breathed, 'even the kitchen has ocean views.'

Modeen smiled and handed her a cup. 'C'mon, let's have these out on the balcony. That's where the *best* views are.'

After pointing out some of the more obvious Gold Coast landmarks from the penthouse's wrap-around balcony, Modeen motioned for them to take a seat on the outdoor lounge.

With a satisfied, 'Ahh,' Hannah sank into a thickly padded chair and sipped her tea. 'Nice, love. Now, what time are you leaving?'

'The plane leaves at eighteen forty-five and arrives in Cairns at twenty-one fifteen. I haven't booked a return flight yet, but at this stage it's likely I'll be there until the end of the week.'

Hannah's brow furrowed. 'Hang on … eighteen forty-five?'

'Sorry Aunty Hann, old habits. You just need to subtract twelve.' When her aunt merely looked at her blankly, she clarified, 'That makes it six forty-five. Pm.'

'Six forty-five pm.' Hannah nodded and gave her niece an angelic smile. 'There now, was that so hard?'

———

Modeen stowed her custom aluminium case in the overhead locker and took her aisle seat. Set up to carry the maximum number of passengers in what was considered to be reasonable comfort, the Airbus A320 offered limited leg room, especially for passengers of above average height. After folding her five foot eleven frame into the cramped space and buckling herself into the seat, Modeen took solace from knowing the flight to Cairns would only take a little over two hours.

From across the aisle a few rows back, a pair of dark eyes roved over her, taking in her short platinum-blonde hair, the smooth, clear skin of her cheek and neck, white designer T-shirt over a firm but undeniably female chest, and snug-fitting cream cargo pants. He licked his lips.

*That's one attractive woman.*

He saw more of her face when she glanced up at the flight attendant doing the pre-flight safety presentation. But on glimpsing the small, barely visible blemish on her cheek, the licentious glint in his eyes vanished, replaced by a frown.

*Attractive alright, but also somehow familiar….*

Taking care to look the other way, he pulled out his mobile phone and hastily flicked through the photographs folder. His searching finger stopped abruptly at a picture of five soldiers. Dressed in camouflage fatigues, they stood at ease, smiling at the camera, combat helmets and weapons held loosely by their sides. Pinching his fingers together on the screen, he flicked them apart to zoom into the middle member of the group. A tall, shapely blonde with a fresh scar on her cheek filled the screen. Glancing across the aisle at Modeen again, he gave a satisfied grunt.

'Is your mobile in flight mode, sir?' A passing eagle-eyed attendant pointed to his phone. 'We're about to take off.'

Smiling up at her, he made a show of doing as she asked before slipping his phone into a pocket, putting his head back and closing his eyes.

Across the aisle, Modeen shifted uneasily in her seat. Recognising the prickle on the back of her neck as her radar kicking in, she peered up and down the aisle. When her glance fell on a dark-skinned man sitting a few rows behind with his eyes closed, she took in his muscular frame in black cargo pants and khaki shirt and thought, *ex-military*. After considering him for a long moment, she settled back in her seat. Picking up her phone, which was already in flight mode, she flicked through the recent text messages. Finding the latest one from Ben, she recalled his words on assigning her the mission.

'JD, I need you in Cairns to assist the Federal Police during the forthcoming premier's visit. It appears Nigel Inslay Olman has ruffled a lot of feathers.'

'He certainly has.' Modeen had given a snort. 'Giving rise to the nickname Nigel No-Friends.'

She'd heard the faint amusement in Ben's voice as he continued with the briefing.

'He's made a lot of enemies since coming into office. Among other things, he put families on the bread line by ordering the sacking of thousands of public servants. Add to that his strong-arm tactics against criminal bikie gangs and the act he established which basically outlaws *all* gangs – the bad and the good – in Queensland, and you've got a volatile mix.

'So be careful, JD, I wouldn't be surprised if there's a contract or two out on him. Unless they've hired a professional, I reckon every gang member from the Rebels, Hells Angels, Coffin Cheaters – you name it – will be out for blood. I wouldn't put it past a few disgruntled public servants to take a shot at him either.'

Two hours later the Airbus slowly broke through the clouds.

'This is First Officer Shaw speaking. We're beginning our descent into Cairns, where the temperature is a steamy thirty-two degrees with humidity at eighty-two percent. We'll be touching down on schedule at twenty-one fifteen. On behalf of Captain Young and the crew, we'd like to thank you for flying with us today.'

After the plane trundled to its assigned gate and its jet engines whined to a halt, Modeen waited until the seatbelt sign was switched off before rising to her feet. Taking a moment to stretch her cramped body, she opened the overhead locker and removed her case before waiting patiently in line to disembark. Once inside the terminal building, she headed to the luggage carousel and retrieved her khaki duffel.

Making her way into the darkness outside, she felt the tropical humidity enfold her like a warm blanket as she joined the long queue at the taxi rank.

A few metres behind, a tall African American male sauntered from the terminal, a duffel slung over one shoulder and a phone pressed to his ear. Stopping outside the entrance, he took his bearings and spotted Modeen standing in the taxi queue. Glancing toward the passenger pick-up zone, he saw a black Chrysler sedan flash its lights and then slink forward in the queue of cars. Setting off with a long-legged stride, he made his way to the vehicle.

Opening the back door, he heaved his duffel onto the seat and then climbed in next to the driver.

Barely glancing at the man, he barked, 'Wait here. I want you to follow a taxi.'

The driver gave a curt shake of his head. 'No can do, Eli. The "Parking Nazis"…,' and he tilted his head toward an official-looking man in a high viz vest already heading their way, '… won't allow us to hang around.'

With a grunt of frustration, Eli waved the driver onward. 'Fine. We'll wait down the road.'

. . .

'The Rydges Hotel in Grafton Street, thanks.' Modeen loaded her duffel and case onto the taxi's back seat and, eyeing the driver, slipped into the passenger seat next to him.

The dark-skinned man merely nodded at her, his curly black beard bobbing with his turbaned head while he focused on punching the destination into his GPS.

Modeen raised an eyebrow at him. 'New to Cairns?'

Muttering, 'Dis my second day,' in a thick middle-eastern accent, the man continued stabbing his finger on the apparently uncooperative GPS.

Modeen sighed and buckled her seatbelt. 'Don't bother with that, I know the way.'

Flicking her a glance, the driver gave up and put both hands on the wheel. Hastily checking the rear view mirror, he pulled into the long line of vehicles leaving the airport. After negotiating a couple of roundabouts, he settled into the drive to the city on Airport Avenue.

When they passed the wetlands viewing platform on the left, a black sedan turned on its lights and pulled out from where it had been parked. It proceeded to follow the taxi at a discreet distance as it turned down Lake Street and into the heavier city traffic.

While Modeen paid the taxi driver, the black Chrysler cruised slowly past, only to pull to the kerb a short distance on. In the front seat, Eli Washington watched Modeen make her way into the hotel's reception area. He waited fifteen minutes and then got out of the car and sauntered to the hotel.

Fronting up to the reception counter, he bestowed a wide smile on the young receptionist.

'Jo Modeen's expecting me, but she forgot to give me her room number. I wonder … would you mind helping me out?'

The receptionist gazed up at him and then smiled shyly back. When he leaned closer and winked at her, she gave a coquettish titter and tapped the keyboard in front of her. 'What name was it again?'

Pronouncing the name slowly, 'Jo Moh-Deen,' Washington craned his neck until he could see the computer screen. 'Spelt M O D E E N.'

The receptionist murmured, 'I don't see….'

But Washington had.

The last entry on the register showed *Josephine Bennett, Room 805*.

'I'm sorry, sir, we don't have anyone here by that name.' The receptionist looked up at him and fluttered her eyelashes. 'Perhaps she's at one of our other hotels? We have three in Cairns, the Esplanade Resort, the Tradewinds, and this one, the Cairns Plaza Hotel.'

'Ahh, of course.' Washington slapped his head. 'I must have the wrong hotel, sorry to bother you. Thanks.' With a smile and a wave, he turned and strode out of the hotel.

Back in the Chrysler, the driver barked, 'Where to now?'

Washington said tightly, 'Did you bring my kit?'

'Nah, it's back at the base. I didn't think you'd need it. Olman doesn't arrive for another two days.'

'I didn't think I'd need it either.' Washington's eyes glinted wickedly. 'But now it appears I might get in some target practice beforehand.'

'Won't that jeopardise the mission?'

Seeing the driver's frown, Washington gave a bark of laughter and thumped him on the shoulder. 'Ah, but like you said, our target doesn't arrive for two days. And if *another* target lands in my lap in the meantime, who am I to waste that opportunity?'

# CHAPTER FOUR

Arriving at the ASIO facility on Swan Island just off the coast of Victoria, NatSec Beta Team leader Ben Smith headed straight to the conference room. There he found the Director General and a handful of the security organisation's regional directors seated around an oval table made entirely of silky oak. They paused in their intense discussions to stare, one with open hostility, as Ben entered the room and pulled out a chair at the end of the table.

At six foot four, and with his muscular physique obvious under a black business suit, he stood out among the other career pen-pushers in the room. Undoing the buttons on his coat, revealing a crisp white business shirt beneath, he eased himself into the chair and returned their nods of greeting.

One man didn't bother with a greeting or pleasantries of any kind. Leaning forward to thump his elbows on the table, he barked an introduction of sorts. 'Director in charge of Western Australian Operations.' Having caught Ben's attention, he said curtly, 'You've put us in a hell of a situation, Smith. One of our field agents is dead thanks to your intel.'

Leaning back in his chair, Ben fixed the man with a level gaze. 'I'm interested to hear how this is NatSec's fault?'

The speaker smacked the table with an open hand. 'You should've warned us of the imminent risk! Our agent was acting on NatSec intel.'

'You have my condolences, of course,' Ben said evenly, 'it's never easy losing a team member, under any circumstances. But correct me if I'm wrong,' and he too leaned forward to rest his arms on the table, 'your field agents are unarmed, are they not? And their main role is to investigate and gather intelligence? NOT to intercept, NOT to detain or apprehend suspects?'

The WA Director's face reddened. 'Don't try to change the subject. You should've warned us this might happen—'

'This isn't helping,' the Director General cut-in, lifting a hand to stop the flow of recriminations. 'Look, what's done is done. What *I* want to know is how we're going to prevent something like this from happening again.'

'Training,' Ben announced without preamble. 'Gathering intel always has the potential to lead to high risk situations, for which your people need to be alert and prepared.'

The WA Director frowned, clearly exasperated. 'Are you saying our field agents should be armed? That throwing more weaponry into the mix is the answer to every difficult situation? Because if you are—'

Ben raised a hand. 'That's not what I'm saying at all. But if you *did* decide to arm your agents, they'd obviously need extensive training before being sent out in the field.'

He sighed and shook his head. 'I'm uncertain what led to Dylan's death, but I assume his cover was blown.'

Another at the table piped up. 'Maybe we should have agents double-up in the field at all times?' At those words, everyone looked at the Director General, who in turn looked expectantly at Ben.

'That may help … depending on the situation.' Ben rubbed his chin thoughtfully. 'But on the other hand you could be placing two agents at risk. I'd suggest having different strategies for domestic and terrorist operations. On the domestic front, the police could be enlisted to assist. At least they're armed and have the power to arrest and detain. On a terrorist level, the Police Tactical Group, NatSec, the military, all have highly skilled operatives available for rapid deployment.'

He paused and then addressed the Director General. 'But for now, I think the question that needs to be asked is who gave your field agent the order to proceed.'

The WA Director's head shot up. Throwing himself back in his chair, he snapped, 'Operational information like that is *classified*, and will only be provided on a need-to-know basis.'

'Yes, and *I* need to know,' the Director General barked back at him. 'I want a full report on everything we have on this, and I mean *everything*.' Turning to Ben, he nodded and said gruffly, 'Thank you for your time and input, Mr Smith. I now have a better grasp of the situation, and will soon ...,' and he threw the WA Director a significant glance, '... have a comprehensive report on which to act.'

————

Modeen woke early the following morning. After a workout in the hotel's gym, she showered and dressed in corporate wear, navy trousers and matching polo top. Heading to the restaurant adjacent to the lobby, she grabbed a quick breakfast and then freshened up in her room and phoned for a taxi, which arrived promptly at the hotel.

Fifteen minutes later she was sitting in the entrance foyer of the Federal Police building, awaiting her o-nine hundred appointment with Chief Superintendent Warwick Sullivan.

In the brightly-lit foyer, security cameras hung from

opposite corners, and a thick wall of double-glazed glass extended from the information counter to the ceiling. A solid hardwood door fitted with a swipe card key lock completed the imposing barrier.

Finding nothing of interest in the magazine she was flicking through, Modeen turned at the sound of approaching male voices. Four police officers, two uniformed and two in plain clothes, carried on their animated conversation as they entered from the street and walked to the centre of the foyer, where they stood with their backs to Modeen.

A few minutes later a loud metallic buzz was heard, and a tall federal officer entered the foyer through the security door.

He announced, 'The Chief will see you now,' and stepped aside while holding the door open.

The four police officers began to move toward him, only to pause and frown when they noticed Modeen rise and join them. One of them moved toward her, raising a halting hand.

When the federal officer said, 'She's with us,' the policeman in the lead dipped his head and made way for her.

They were led to a small conference room, where a tall, silver-haired man wearing a dark blue suit and a serious expression rose to greet them. Clusters of crowns and pips decorated the lapels of his jacket, and the top right pocket was covered in ribbons and medals.

Modeen swallowed a grin. If she hadn't known better, she might've mistaken him for a five star general.

Indicating the chairs around the conference table, he said without smiling, 'Please, take a seat, and thanks for your promptness.' He waited just long enough for them to settle before launching into the briefing. 'As most of you are aware, I'm Chief Superintendent Warwick Sullivan, and am tasked with the security detail for Premier Olman's visit to Cairns tomorrow. This morning's meeting is to plan how we can best deploy resources to ensure the premier's safety and that of his entourage.'

Sullivan indicated Modeen with a sweep of his open hand. 'NatSec agent Josephine Bennet will be working with us as a specialist consultant.'

The youngest uniformed officer had been eyeing her sceptically. Now he cracked his knuckles, leaned forward and said with a sardonic tilt to his lips, 'Sergeant Bellamy, QPS. And what is your specialisation, Ms Bennet?'

Modeen returned his gaze levelly. 'Counter-terrorism.'

'I see.' Raising a mocking eyebrow, he ran his eyes over her. 'And I suppose you learnt that from some university text book.' He didn't wait for her to respond before puffing out his chest and going on. 'Look, we deal with *real* people and *real* situations every day. Our strategies and training aren't simply theoretical, taken from the pages of *Counter-terrorism for Dummies,* or some such book.'

Grinning, he looked to the other men expecting to find them joining in the laughter. Instead he was met by grave, in some cases reproachful, expressions and his grin faded.

Sullivan glared at him. 'Ms Bennet comes highly recommended by her agency, and I expect *all* officers dealing with her to be *courteous* and *respectful.*'

One of the other men had already extended a hand to Modeen from across the table. 'I'm Senior Sergeant Kevin Simpson, and beside me is first officer Gavin Rogers.' Simpson continued speaking as they shook hands. 'We're from the Police Tactical Group Brisbane, part of a team of six who'll be working with you tomorrow. In PTG, we're trained to deal with domestic counter-terrorism and hostage rescue.'

He paused to eye Bellamy. 'And for the record I understand that national security agents, such as Ms Bennet, are highly trained operatives, often hand-picked from the elite forces.' Simpson gave Modeen a respectful dip of his head.

She returned the nod. 'That was certainly correct in my case. I was recruited after leaving the SASR, where I served in Afghanistan, Iraq, Tizak and East Timor...,' and she threw Bellamy an amused glance, '... where they fire at you with *real* bullets.' She sobered. 'However, I believe our focus today is on security, and it's my understanding that all useful and unbiased input will be tabled.' Seeing Sullivan's prompt nod of agreement, she concluded, 'We need to cover all the bases to ensure the best possible outcome.'

'Well said, Ms Bennet.' The chief narrowed his eyes at Bellamy. 'Now let's get down to business.' After tapping on his computer keyboard, he turned to check the large screen on the wall behind him. When it remained blank, he frowned and looked back at his laptop. Rubbing his chin, he glanced hopefully at the projector and shook his head.

Modeen sat forward. 'Is that laptop a Dell running Windows Eight?'

Sullivan nodded his head distractedly.

'Try pressing *Function* and *F8.*'

This time Sullivan looked at her, but with a blank expression.

Rising to stand in front of his laptop, she murmured, 'Sometimes this works,' and pressed the *Fn* and *F8* keys. A second later the screen blinked and Olman's itinerary popped up.

A relieved Sullivan gave a ghost of a smile. 'Thank you, Ms Bennet.' Taking a moment to spread a large map of Cairns on the table, he traced a finger over a zigzagging line highlighted in fluoro yellow. 'This is the planned route.'

Then he pointed to the itinerary on the screen. 'Olman arrives at eleven hundred hours and goes direct from the airport to Cairns Base Hospital, where he's opening the new wing. En route the premier's high security 7-series sedan will be escorted by two TPG armoured Toyota Landcruisers, and two motorcycle policemen. At twelve-thirty he'll be lunching in his presidential suite at the Pullman International.'

At the mention of a presidential suite, Bellamy gave a snort.

Ignoring him, Sullivan kept his eyes down and continued. 'From fourteen hundred to fifteen thirty Olman will meet with the Mayor and CEO at the council chambers, after which he will return to the Pullman. From nineteen hundred to twenty-one thirty, he'll dine in a private function room of the Pullman with the member for Cairns and other dignitaries.' Sullivan sat back to glance around the table. 'Thus ending his first day.'

'Right, let's start with the airport.' Modeen leaned forward to get a better look at the map. 'Is Olman arriving on a Government jet, domestic flight, or by private charter?'

―――――

The late model M3 BMW, arranged for Modeen's use by NatSec's resource manager Leanne Martin, was parked outside the federal office. The meeting had lasted most of the day, so it was late afternoon by the time she collected the car and headed to her hotel.

Swiping her key card to unlock the door of her room, she dumped her work bag on the floor beside the bed and went straight to the kitchenette to fill and switch on the kettle. While waiting for it to boil, she undressed, gratefully tossing her work clothes onto the bed. After slipping into a light cotton shirt and denim shorts, she retrieved the aluminium case from the bottom of her wardrobe and placed it on the coffee table. Thumbing the combination lock, she clicked the lid open.

Hearing the kettle switch itself off, she made herself a coffee and took it out onto the balcony to take in the views. The moment she opened the sliding glass doors she was hit by the noise of city bustle – sirens, traffic, beeping horns, voices – and the warm embrace of the thick, humid air.

Moving to the railing, she leaned on her forearms, sipping her coffee and taking in the vista. She watched lights flicker on in surrounding high-rises as the sun disappeared behind the lush green hills of the Cairns hinterland.

A short way down the street at the Cairns Reef Casino, a tall, dark-skinned man entered the elevator and made his way to the twenty metre high rooftop dome. After paying his entry fee, he sauntered through the dome's tropical garden, feigning interest in the wildlife enclosures he passed. Skirting around the crocodile enclosure in the centre of the display, he headed toward the flying fox amusement ride and then paused.

After taking a quick glance around, he slipped

behind a thick bed of crimson-trunked lipstick palms and out through the service door behind them. Once on the outer balcony, he pushed his way through the forest of green foliage that circled the entire dome, heading to the western side of the building, checking the view every metre or so. Finding a spot with clear sight of the Rydges Hotel, he took up position. Taking the tinted aviator Raybans from off the top of his head and slipping them over his eyes, he watched the final crest of the sun sink behind the mountains.

He remained still for a long moment, listening carefully. As soon as he was sure he hadn't been made, he took the backpack from his shoulders and began assembling the sniper rifle. After fitting the silencer and Night Force US Optics scope, he shoved his sunglasses back on top of his close-cropped head and put a pair of range finder binoculars to his eyes.

*Distance confirmed – six hundred and fifty metres.*

His target was sitting at a balcony table, gazing out at the city's backdrop of green hills. Lifting his head, he felt for wind direction but there was no movement of air at all.

Setting down the binoculars, he gave a disdainful snort.

*Too easy!*

Pressing the butt of the rifle into his shoulder and peering through the scope, he placed the cross hairs on the back of his target's head. Keeping his body motionless and his breathing shallow, he squeezed the trigger.

And let loose one .300 Winchester Magnum round.

Modeen tipped her mug to swallow the last of her coffee when her phone chimed. As she leaned forward to grab it from off the outdoor table, her ears caught the sound of a high-pitched whine and she felt a rush of air above her bent head. As the sliding glass door to her unit exploded in a cloud of shards and glass dust, her training kicked in.

Rolling onto the floor, she flattened out and ducked to the opposite side of the balcony, pushing open what remained of the sliding door as she went. Bracing herself against the railing for a split second, she leapt forward like a runner on the starting blocks and dived diagonally through the doorway. Completing a forward roll at the coffee table, she snatched the Walther PPQ from out of the aluminium case and sprang to her feet.

Moving swiftly toward the door, she grabbed the tea towel from off the kitchen bench and wrapped the pistol in it.

In the elevator on the way down, she calculated the ballistics in her head.

*A high-powered weapon.*

*I was facing west and the shot came from my seven o'clock.*

She'd felt the rush of air and heard the projectile

whistle past right where her head had been the briefest of moments before.

*The shooter had to've been somewhere in the vicinity of the casino, in or on a building of roughly the same level as my apartment.*

The instant the elevator doors swished open, she shot out into the lobby, startling a pair of elderly tourists standing waiting for the lift. Throwing them a hasty, 'Sorry, 'scuse me,' she sprinted out the left side entrance onto Crofton Street. Turning the corner into Spence Street, she lengthened her stride and headed toward the casino.

Dashing through the traffic and weaving between cars and pedestrians, she crossed Lake Street onto Abbot, where she stopped to glance back at the Rydges Hotel and her unit on the eighth floor. The shooter must have been positioned on the casino's roof or in one of the apartments to the right of it.

It only took a quick scan of the roof line of the Galleria and Louis Vuitton building to know it was too far to the left, and wouldn't have provided a clear shot.

She sprinted around the corner and propped. In the distance a familiar-looking dark-skinned man jogged down the casino's rear steps. Swinging a backpack across his broad shoulders, he turned and loped up the footpath toward the shipping terminal.

As Modeen took off toward him, he straddled a waiting motorcycle. Although rapidly closing the distance, she could only watch as the bike roared into life and took off down the street toward the wharf, its rear wheel leaving a black line of rubber on the bitumen. When the rider leaned the retro-shaped bike low around the next corner, Modeen glimpsed a flash of white on red.

*Bold white writing on a red tank ... gotta be a Ducati.*

# CHAPTER FIVE

The roar of the Ducati's motor was a faint hum in the distance by the time Modeen reached the casino's rear entrance. She made her way up the stairs to the rooftop dome and flashed her NatSec ID at the young attendant, whose eyes widened on seeing the official badge.

Entering the wildlife compound, Modeen skirted the enclosures, checking behind each one, until she located a service door leading onto the outer balcony. The door wasn't properly latched and swung open at her touch.

Stepping outside, she moved quietly, listening for any movement. Pushing her way past the thick foliage, she stopped at a point where she had an uninterrupted view of the Rydges Hotel. Glancing around, she noted some disturbance in the vegetation, but nothing else to indicate the shot had been taken from that location. She checked the height and angle. Both seemed right, and the setting sun would have been too low behind the mountains to affect the shooter's vision.

*Still wouldn't have been my first pick of locations.*

There was nothing else to do but return to her apartment. She did so with mixed feelings, relief she'd dodged a bullet – literally – and disappointment the assailant had given her the slip.

*He caught me unawares ... obviously my radar has its limits.*

Back in her glass-splattered room, she pulled the thick curtains across the windows and shattered sliding door and then checked her mobile. One missed call, from Ben. After pressing the phone's touch screen to return his call, she unwrapped her pistol from the tea towel and placed it back in the aluminium case.

Her call was answered on the first ring.

Ben's words were clipped, precise. 'Sit rep, JD.'

'I met with Warwick Sullivan this morning at the federal police headquarters, and have a briefing with the Police Tactical Group tomorrow. Security for Olman at this stage looks good, however there's been a development that may or may not be related.'

'Yes?'

'There was an African American male on the plane with me yesterday who caught my attention. I got the distinct impression he was ex-military. I believe this is the same individual who took a shot at me this evening.'

'Took a *shot* at you?' Ben's voice rose. 'Are you alright?'

'I'm OK, the glass door of my eighth floor apartment at the Rydges copped the worst of it. I was on the balcony having a coffee when the shot came, I believe from the vicinity of the casino.' When her phone buzzed with an incoming text she held it out and glanced at a photo of the same dark-skinned man on the screen. She put the phone against her ear once more. 'That's him. Who is he, and how did you know it was him?'

'Just a hunch. He's a Yank using the alias Eli Washington, but his real name's Jackson Foster. You're right, he's ex-Army, but now freelances as a hired thug, slash hit man. ASIO have been tracking his movements, and I doubt his being in Cairns at the same time as Olman is a coincidence.'

'But if he was after Olman why would he blow his cover by taking a shot at me?' Modeen frowned. 'And why does his name sound familiar?'

'When Gator went MIA in Afghanistan, Foster and his associate Kyle Davidson, AKA Jon Reger, were the two soldiers who went missing with him. Their bodies were never recovered.' Ben paused before continuing with a thread of emotion in his deep voice. 'And we know how that turned out for Gator.'

Her phone buzzed again with the arrival of another

photo, this time featuring a tall, heavily-built man. Dressed in stained blue jeans and a checked flannel shirt, sleeves rolled up to his brawny elbows, he looked like a lumberjack.

'Reger,' Ben said curtly. 'Don't let the flannel shirt fool you, he's hard-core military, just like Foster.'

'So these guys have come under the spotlight?'

Ben gave a grunt. 'After discovering Gator was alive, I assumed they were too. I also assumed they were in cahoots, so I asked ASIO to follow up on them.'

'What did they find?'

'Reason to believe my assumption was correct.' Ben sighed. 'I sent Spooky to check on an ASIO agent who went missing while tailing Foster. He was found at Kingstown Barracks on Rottnest Island with his throat cut. From their tracks, Spook believes there were three insurgents who bugged out of there by boat.' Ben paused. 'Now we know Foster's in Cairns, I'm sending Spook and Wolf to join you there. With a bit of luck you might come up with some leads on this case.' He paused again, and Modeen could almost hear him thinking.

'If Foster and Reger were in with Gator, then Foster might have been vying for some payback.' A grim note crept into Ben's voice. 'The second, worse scenario is that there's a price on our heads. So stay alert, JD, he might try again.'

Recalling the image of her assailant roaring away

on the motorcycle, Modeen said sharply, 'Foster got away on a red Ducati Monster.'

'Monster? So … a big bike?'

She gave a wry snort. 'Monster is its designation. You know, like a Corvette can be a Stingray, or an Alfa Romeo a Spider? I think this was a late model Ducati Monster Eight Twenty-One.'

'Your point being?'

'Well, there aren't too many of them in Australia let alone in far north Queensland. It shouldn't be hard to come up with some rego numbers and addresses.'

'Good work JD, I'll get on it. In the meantime, your priority is still Olman. Organise yourself some alternate accommodation and I'll send a crew to clean up the damage to the Rydges apartment. Wolf and Spooky will be there ASAP.'

'Right.'

After packing her kit, she took a minute to make another call. It too was answered on the first ring.

'Resources, Leanne speaking.'

'Hi Leanne, it's Jo Bennet. Could you book me into the Pullman International in Abbott Street, Cairns please?' She heard a pen scratching on paper at the other end of the call. 'I need a room facing the harbour overlooking the casino, preferably around the sixth floor level, or higher if possible. And could you tell me when Spoo— I mean, when Luke Williams and Troy Ryan are expected to arrive in Cairns?'

Leanne's tone was all business. 'Mr Williams is

booked on a direct flight from Perth, arriving in Cairns at o-four hundred tomorrow. Mr Ryan's ETA from Canberra is twenty-four hundred tonight. I haven't booked their accommodation yet, should I put them in the Pullman as well?'

'Yes, preferably on the same level, and with at least one apartment facing west toward the mountains.'

'I'll text you when I have booking confirmations. Now, do you need anything else?'

'That's all for the moment, thanks Leanne.'

———

At ten minutes past midnight, Troy Wolverton strode through the Cairns airport lounge toward baggage collection. From under heavy brows his almost-black, thickly lashed eyes swept his surroundings, on the search for anything out of the ordinary.

Dressed casually in blue jeans and white T-shirt, he'd let his dark hair grow out of the Army regulation crew cut into an unruly 'who cares' style.

Arriving at the baggage carousel, he checked the fight arrivals on the display and took up position near the rubber curtained entry to the conveyor, to wait for his duffel to appear. Standing there, appearing unconcerned but still very much aware of his surroundings, he caught a glimpse of a tall woman making her way toward him.

The woman's auburn hair was cut in a stylish bob,

and she wore jeans and a floral blouse. She also had on a suede battle jacket, which seemed a little out of place to Wolf, who'd felt the tropical humidity when crossing the airport's tarmac. He grew still, and waited.

Coming to stand close beside him, the woman placed a hand on his shoulder and whispered, 'How was your flight, Mr Ryan?'

A grin tugged at the corners of his firm mouth as he turned to hold her at arms length. 'You sure do have some different looks, Mrs Ryan.' He smiled into her China blue eyes and pulled her in for a hug. Feeling the hard lump of a shoulder holster and pistol beneath her jacket, his expression became serious.

Sensing her inner tension, he pressed her closer against him. 'Why the disguise?' he said in her ear, his tone low and gruff and his breath hot against her skin. 'And what's with packin' Walt for a simple airport pick-up?'

'Let's just say I'm being cautious and don't want to attract any more attention tonight.'

Feeling her withdraw a little, he relaxed his grip but kept his hands on her arms while taking a quick scan around them. 'What's happened?'

'Grab your bag and I'll brief you on the way.' She tilted her head toward the conveyor as a bulky duffel emerged through the curtains. 'We'll be back here at o-four hundred to collect Spook.'

———

The arrivals hall was deserted and eerily quiet when Modeen and Wolf once more made their way to the baggage carousel. They checked the screen mounted above it, which flashed details of the Perth flight's arrival as muffled sounds reached their ears. The double glass doors securing the departures lounge from the arrivals hall swished open as the first bleary-eyed passengers trickled through.

Wolf bent to say against her ear, 'You see him?'

'See who?'

The voice came from behind them. Whirling around, they found Spooky grinning up at them.

'Jesus, Spook,' Wolf snapped as they fist-bumped.

Spooky's grin widened and he turned to Modeen. 'And who do we have here?' He waggled his eyebrows at her.

She returned his grin. 'Good to see ya, Spook.' When she moved in to hug him, he promptly placed his briefcase at his feet and hugged her warmly back.

'What's with the disguise Modeen?' He threw Wolf a roguish wink. 'Or shouldn't I ask?'

'Humph!' Raising a lazy eyebrow, Wolf drawled, 'Come on, grab your bag. We'll brief you on the way.'

———

Back in Modeen's room at the Pullman International, Spooky finished his account of the events on Rottnest Island.

Wolf regarded him levelly. 'How did ASIO know Foster was based there?'

'They didn't. After Ben found out Gator was alive, he alerted ASIO, and they began an investigation into the whereabouts of the other two soldiers who'd gone MIA with Gator. They got hold of their military mug shots and used facial recognition software to help with the search. When Foster's face was ID'd at the Fremantle markets, ASIO assigned an agent to tail him. The poor bastard ended up at Kingstown Barracks on Rotto … with his throat cut.'

'But Foster's a Yank isn't he?' Modeen began pacing the floor. 'So what was he doing in Gator's squad in the first place?'

'According to Ben, Foster was a green beret with the Tenth Special Forces Group out of Fort Carson, Colorado. He was seconded to the ADF under an exchange program as part of our alliance with the US. He apparently had form as a civilian in the states. Before joining up he was into people smuggling, drugs, and general racketeering on the black market. Ben suspects Foster of introducing Gator to Batista, through his connections.'

'So Foster's the ring leader?' As he spoke, Wolf rose to make his way to the unit's kitchenette and pour himself a glass of water.

'No, apparently the three of them formed a syndicate. But when Gator and Reger, the two with the biggest egos had a falling out,' and Spooky rolled his eyes, 'Foster sided with Reger, who also had form before enlisting. His links with Melbourne's underbelly were only discovered after Ben opened the case. Anyway, Reger and Foster have combined forces to build their own business, cashing in on contracts here and there. And that brings us to Olman.'

Spooky fixed Modeen with an intense gaze. 'But I'm guessing that's not why you're packing Walt, and why you've got the curtains drawn and the lights dimmed.'

'No.' Modeen stopped pacing to stand by the kitchen counter and return his gaze. 'Foster was on the plane when I flew into Cairns, and now I'm certain it was him that took a shot at me yesterday evening.'

Beside her, Wolf's hand holding the tumbler paused midway to his mouth as his whole body tensed.

Spooky's eyes widened. 'He shot at you? Why, were you tailing him?'

'No, I didn't find out who he was until afterwards.' She gave a humourless grin. 'I was on my balcony at the Rydges, having a coffee and minding my own business. After the shot, I ran down to the casino and saw him take off on a red, late model Ducati.'

Setting down the glass with a thump, Wolf scowled and barked, 'Did you get the numberplate?'

'No, but Ben was able to track the bike down anyway. It'd been reported stolen from a local motorcycle shop. He retrieved security footage from a camera at the rear of the casino, and the bike shop owner was able to ID the Duke. The Police later found it abandoned at Wrights Creek, just off the highway heading south.'

'That doesn't help us any.' Spooky leaned forward to cup his face in his hands.

Modeen shook her head. 'No, but at least we know who we're up against. And there's something else. Ben thinks Foster may've taken the shot at me as payback for what we did to Gator and Batista. Or worse, that the terrorist organisation Spear of Allah has placed a bounty on our heads.'

'Bring it on,' Wolf growled, his dark eyes glinting.

'So we need to watch our backs,' Spooky muttered. 'Situation normal.'

Modeen nodded. 'Yes, we have to stay sharp to keep Olman *and* each other safe.' She glanced down at her watch. 'It's o-five hundred, we should try to catch some sleep. Rendezvous back here at eight when we'll grab some breakfast and go over the details for Olman's arrival. We're meeting the Feds at the airport at ten-thirty. They'll issue us with security passes and go over the last minute details.'

Rising to his feet Spooky looked at Wolf, who kept his eyes fixed on Modeen and made no move to leave. With a quizzical frown, Spooky announced, 'Right then. Well, I'll see you both at o-eight hundred.' As he left the unit he flicked another glance at Wolf, whose expression grew more intense as he closed the distance between himself and Modeen.

As the door swung closed behind him, Spooky made his way thoughtfully down the corridor to his room.

# CHAPTER SIX

I n the lobby of the Pullman International, Coco's restaurant buzzed with business people and bright-eyed holiday makers alike preparing to start their day.

Carrying a tray of coffee, poached eggs and warm buttered toast, Modeen made her way through the bustle to a secluded table in the far back corner of the restaurant. Taking her seat between Wolf and Spooky, who were busy emptying their own heaped plates, she licked her lips and unloaded her tray. Still chewing, Spooky sat back to eye her over his coffee mug.

'So basically, Olman arrives at eleven hundred, opens a wing at the hospital, visits the council chambers, and then overnights in this hotel?' Looking to Modeen for confirmation, he took a long sip of his espresso.

She nodded. 'He's booked himself into the presidential suite on the top floor.'

Wolf gave a grunt and raised his head. 'That little arsehole's got tickets on himself.' He went back to eating after first mumbling, 'Classic case of small man's disease.'

'Yeah.' Spooky grinned, clearly untroubled by the fact he was the shortest of the three at the table. 'Apparently he used to be a CO in the army and was known for alienating himself from his subordinates. Seems he doesn't like associating with the riff-raff.'

Modeen threw him a rueful smile. 'Well, it doesn't appear anything's changed.' She shook her head. 'Apart from his own personal bodyguards, he'll be escorted every step of the way by federal officers, and the regular police will be manning road blocks and providing extra security.' She paused to pop a forkful of poached egg and toast into her mouth, and drained her cup before going on.

'Before he gets here we'll need to go over his route from the airport and see if we can spot any holes in the security. The Feds will provide us with comms units so we can keep track of any deviations to the plan. He's also holding a private function for some select politicians and dignitaries here, tonight, so we're in for a long day.'

Flicking the two men a significant glance, she picked up her cup and returned to the buffet to recharge her coffee.

————

Preceded by two burly bodyguards, and at five foot four barely visible behind them, Nigel Olman exited the Gulfstream G4 charter jet at Cairns airport.

The guards took position, one behind and the other in front of their diminutive boss, as they went down the stairway and climbed into the high security 7-series BMW waiting on the tarmac with its engine running and air-con on high.

As soon as his passengers were settled, the driver accelerated away from the whining-down jet, escorted by two motorcycle police and two black PTG V8 Land-cruisers.

From her position on the roof of the airport terminal, Modeen lowered her sniper rifle to watch Wolf join the convoy. The two PTG officers stationed on the roof with her kept their rifles at the ready while watching the vehicles disappear down Airport Avenue.

As soon as they were out of sight, the three moved in unison, packing up their gear and preparing to follow the procession.

From their perch on the roof of the Cairns Base Hospital, Spooky and two other federal officers watched the convoy approach. One of the officer's two-ways squawked with another report on the vehicles' progress through a check point along the way. Spooky sighed, thinking, *it was all hurry up and wait in the Army, and it still is.*

The arrival of the Government car and its convoy met with excited murmurs from the greeters gathered at the hospital's main entrance. After much hand shaking and gushed welcomes, the premier was led inside, followed closely by his burly minders.

Modeen and the two PTG officers arrived a short time later. They took up watch positions at the back of the throng while Olman, standing on a makeshift stage, puffed out his chest and spoke at length about his efforts to secure the new hospital wing, espousing its long term benefit to the north Queensland community. Glancing around, Modeen couldn't see Wolf anywhere, but she knew he'd be watching from a position with good line of sight.

*Watching, and fully focused on the job at hand, I hope.*

A frown creased her brow.

*Why am I even thinking that? I've never had the slightest cause to worry about his focus on the job before.*

When sudden applause rang out, she snapped to attention. The ceremony was over. With a curt nod to the officers beside her, she made her way to the Pullman International to rendezvous with Wolf and await Olman's arrival there.

At the Pullman she found Wolf standing with Chief Superintendent Warwick Sullivan and two heavily armed members of the PTG. After nodding their greetings, the five of them stood silently watching as the procession of vehicles came into view.

When Modeen flicked Wolf a sideways glance, she found him staring straight ahead, his lips a firm, determined line. And while it wasn't obvious to anyone else, she knew he was aware of her every movement.

The fig tree's enormous leafy canopy provided perfect protection from the glare and harsh rays of the sun. Taking another glance at the sunburnt tourists wandering the Cairns Esplanade, many holding cold cans of drink or dripping ice creams, Jackson Foster smiled and unclipped his backpack. Slinging it to the ground, he sat down and rested his back against the fig tree's massive trunk.

Removing a modified remote control unit from the backpack, he placed it on his lap and slid the power toggle to the ON position. When its ten by eight digital display powered on, he fiddled with the controls, and three hundred and twelve metres away a Phantom Quadcopter's blades whirred into life.

The drone rose slowly from its concealed hiding place on the roof of a federation-style building beside the Pullman International. It hovered vertically, its on-board camera following the procession of vehicles as they pulled off Abbott Street and circled beneath the hotel's impressive front colonnade. As the 7-series BMW came to a halt, the drone began its downward swoop, negotiating several palm trees as it vied for a closer position to its target.

From the lavish marble steps of the hotel's entrance, Modeen caught movement to her left and whirled around. She spied the drone hovering level with the top of a palm tree at a distance of about forty metres, and getting closer.

Throwing, 'Any of you authorise a drone?' over her shoulder at the PTG officers, she waited just long enough to see their shrugs in response before whipping the Walther PPQ from her shoulder holster and in one smooth motion, firing off a single round.

In the sky above, the drone exploded with a deafening boom. Everyone within a thirty metre radius was thrown back by the force of the blast, and glass shattered from nearby windows as fragments of the drone cascaded to the ground in fiery balls of molten metal and plastic.

Yelling into his comms unit, 'Get Olman inside now!' Wolf yanked the Glock from his shoulder holster and raced toward the BMW.

From their vantage point at the top of the stairs Modeen and the PTG officers leapt to their feet again, weapons at the ready, while Wolf reefed open the back door of the BMW and heaved Olman out by his suit collar. Pushing the whimpering premier's head down, Wolf waited until the two bodyguards and two PTG officers took up flanking positions on either side of him before racing up the stairs, using his brawny body to help shield Olman.

As they passed Modeen she slipped in behind them, covering their retreat into the hotel.

Amid gasps and shrieks from hotel staff and guests inside the plush, chandelier-lit foyer, the group with Olman at its centre piled into the first elevator that opened. Wolf reached a burly arm across the others to punch in the number for the floor of the presidential suite and the doors swished closed. Nobody spoke as the lift took them upward, Olman's harsh breathing was the only audible sound. The security detail kept their weapons at the ready, poised for when the doors opened on the top floor.

When they did Wolf stepped out first, leading with his Glock. After checking left and right, he indicated for the others to follow and they made their way along the thickly-carpeted corridor to the presidential suite.

The security guard standing sentry outside the apartment saw them hurrying toward him and hastily opened the door. Inside, Olman's PA rose from where she'd been sitting at the table to gawp at the sight of her boss being half-dragged, half-carried into the room.

Once everyone was safely inside the apartment, Wolf closed and locked the door behind them. Seeing Olman collapse onto the sofa to be fussed over by his PA, Modeen inclined her head at Wolf and they quietly left.

Returning to the scene at the front of the hotel, they found Spooky kneeling over a pile of drone fragments.

Holding up a piece to show them, he said, 'C4 casing,' and got to his feet. 'No wonder it went up with a bang. And over there,' and he pointed to another fragment, 'the barrel of a nine millimetre pistol.' Fixing them with a meaningful glance, he said, 'This drone was modified so it could either take someone out with a single shot, or be used as a Kamikaze to take out a crowd.'

'Nice going.' Wolf thumped Modeen on the back. 'If it had got any closer it could've done some serious damage, not only to Olman but to us as well.'

Modeen nodded. 'We'll get Forensics to examine the pieces, but I think for now we should sweep the immediate area and lock down these buildings. As we know, under perfect line of sight conditions these drones can be controlled from up to two kilometres away. But surrounded by all these structures, I suspect the operator would've been much closer.'

At their nods of agreement, she spoke into her comms unit. 'Chief Sullivan, Jo Bennet here.'

'Go ahead, Bennet.'

'We need every available officer to lock down and search the buildings in the immediate area, including the Pullman, looking for someone carrying a remote control device or just acting suspicious. I also need Forensics to go over the fragments of the drone that exploded in the driveway.'

'Copy that.' From where he stood in Olman's presidential suite, trying to assure a flustered and increasingly outraged premier that the security measures in place *were* sufficient, Sullivan turned to his second in command and barked, 'Make it happen.'

Downstairs, Modeen motioned the others closer as she said quietly, 'Wolf, you're with me. Spook, you check the north. Wolf and I will head back down Abbott Street and peel off to cover the east and west.'

When Spooky nodded and ducked off heading northward, the other two set off at a jog toward the wharf. When they reached the end of the street Wolf pointed west and peeled off that way. Modeen circled around to the front of the Reef Casino and continued on across Spence Street. She paused at the corner of Fogarty Park in front of the pier and scanned to her left.

Sweeping a glance over the lines of people cycling, strolling and jogging along the Esplanade, her attention was caught by a tall, dark-skinned man wearing a backpack, approximately two hundred and fifty metres away.

She set off at a sprint, calling into her comms unit, 'Bennet in pursuit of suspect heading north on the Esplanade.'

A moment later when Foster turned to take a quick, unconcerned check behind, he glimpsed a woman running purposefully toward him. Taking one look at her official-looking clothing, he took off at speed down the path, shoving people out of the way as he ran.

Seeing him dash away, Modeen increased speed and barked into her comms, 'African American male, approximately six two. Black cargo pants, khaki shirt.'

Foster sprinted down the concrete path which turned into a wide timber walkway that stretched north past the man-made lagoon. Taking a hasty glance over his shoulder, he saw Modeen closing the distance, only a hundred metres behind, and weaving in and out of startled pedestrians in her pursuit.

Their eyes met for a brief instant and she considered taking out her pistol, but the path was too crowded for her to risk taking a shot. Ahead of her, Foster appeared to slow his pace as he ran past two heavily built Islanders, who stepped onto the path behind him.

Dressed in black singlets and pants and covered in traditional tribal tattoos, the men began sauntering in Modeen's direction. As she ran past the first man, he snaked out a hand and grabbed her arm. Though startled, she instinctively locked her arm in his and used her momentum to swing him around, sending him careering into his accomplice. The two men thumped into each other face-on and tumbled heavily to the ground. Re-focusing her attention on the fast disappearing Foster, Modeen tried to leap over the pile of fallen flesh but fell flat on her stomach when a burly hand caught her around the ankle.

As the Islander dragged her toward himself, she rolled onto her back and as soon as she was close enough, lashed out with her free foot. The vicious kick to the side of his face had his head snapping sideways as shards of teeth sailed into the air ahead of a dark spurt of blood.

The instant he released his grip on her ankle she sprang nimbly to her feet. Surprising her with their swift agility, the two large men rolled upright.

The first man hacked up a loogie and spat the bloody glob on the ground as he and his colleague advanced on her, grinning wickedly through broken and gappy teeth. But their grins vanished and their eyes widened with shock when Modeen whipped out her PPQ and immediately fired off two shots.

With anguished cries of, 'Ahhh!' her adversaries fell to the ground in unison, both clutching their knee caps. Nearby pedestrians screamed, some cowered where they stood, while others scarpered in all directions.

Shouting, 'Stay!' at her two attackers as though they were a pair of Rottweilers, Modeen shoved her pistol into the waist of her pants and turned to continue her pursuit of Foster.

She ran down the path for another fifty metres and scanned ahead but there was no sign of him. Slowing to a walk, she turned and back-tracked to stand over the two moaning Islanders.

Staring down at them dispassionately, she called over the comms, 'I've lost the suspect but have two detainees in custody. Require an ambulance and security in front of the RSL on the Esplanade, ASAP.'

Kneeling next to the biggest of the two islanders, she pressed the barrel of her PPQ against his temple and snarled in his ear, 'Who are you working for?'

The man blinked up at her and swore.

'Who are you *working* for?' She shoved the barrel in harder, making a pale indent in the skin of his temple.

The man winced and swore again, before muttering belligerently, 'He paid us two hundred bucks a piece for the day.'

'*Who* paid you?' She used her weight to drill his head into the ground. 'Who?'

Crying out with pain, the man curled as though into a foetal position, and stuttered, 'Th-that guy, the one you were chasing. S-said his name was Washington ... Eli Washington.'

When she released some of the pressure against his head, the man brought his injured knee higher to cradle it. Blood oozed between his stubby fingers as he blubbed, 'That's all I know.'

While keeping the pistol against his temple, Modeen released a bit more pressure. 'How did he contact you?'

'At th-the Pussy Cat Club ... on S-spence Street.' The man's breathing was ragged with pain, and he sounded on the verge of tears. 'W-we're bouncers there. He just asked if we wanted to make some extra cash, that's all.'

'Who else was with him?'

'He … he was alone.'

'Put the gun down *now*.'

Glancing over her shoulder, Modeen saw a young police officer fifteen metres away pointing a Glock. She eyed him but remained standing over the man at her feet, the muzzle of her gun still pressed against his head.

Seizing his chance, he extended a pleading hand toward the officer and spat, 'Help! This *bitch* shot me in the knee!'

Modeen said firmly, 'National Security,' and flashed the security pass on the lanyard around her neck. 'Come here and cover these two, I've got an ambulance on the way.'

The officer remained where he stood with his Glock trained on her. 'I said, put the gun down.'

Still eyeing him, Modeen was considering her options when she saw Spooky sidle up behind the officer, one hand resting on the pistol in his shoulder holster.

Leaning in, he said jauntily in the officer's ear, 'I'd do as she says if I were you.' He reached forward to push the officer's gun arm down and stepped between them.

# CHAPTER SEVEN

Modeen and Spooky stood on the wide Esplanade walkway watching the ambos load the two injured men into the back of the ambulance. A police car waited on the verge nearby, its powerful motor idling throatily. As the cumbersome ambulance prepared to accelerate away, Wolf's deep voice came from the walkway behind them.

'Seems Olman's had enough excitement for today. He's cancelled his meeting at the council chambers.'

Modeen turned to him with a one-armed shrug. 'That's not a bad idea. The council building would make a good location for a hit, it's the hardest one to lock down.'

The men nodded.

Coming to stand at Modeen's side, Wolf watched as the ambulance bounced over the curb and motored away, followed closely by the police escort. He nudged her with an elbow. 'So what happened here?'

'I made Foster and gave chase. Two of his hired thugs tried to pull me up.'

Wolf looked down at her with concern and his gravelly voice deepened. 'You OK?'

'Sure, nothing I couldn't handle.'

He was regarding her intently but at her smile his expression lifted. 'Good.' He inclined his head toward the Pullman. 'Sullivan wants us back there for a debrief on the drone.'

Spooky turned to them with a lift of his chin. 'You two go. I'm gonna search the area, just in case Foster's still around or decides to backtrack.' He strode away calling over his shoulder, 'I'll catch up with you later.'

———

As Modeen and Wolf entered the meeting room on the ground floor at the rear of the Pullman International, Kevin Simpson and his 2IC from the PTG, Gavin Rogers, rose to greet them.

Simpson said with a hint of regret in his voice, 'Sorry we missed the fireworks. After we left the hospital I was keen to set up sentries at the council chambers.' His expression brightened and he extended a hand to shake Modeen's. 'By the way, nice shooting, Ms Bennet.'

From where he'd remained seated at the conference

table, a sour-faced Sergeant Bellamy cracked his knuckles, put his hands behind his head and leaned back muttering, 'Pretty reckless if you ask me. I'd hate to think where that bullet would've ended up if you'd missed.'

'Give it a rest, Bellamy.' Simpson threw him a sideways glance as he and Rogers took their seats again.

At the head of the table, Chief Sullivan called the meeting to order. With an appreciative nod at Modeen, he said, 'Nice shooting indeed.' He went on to address the table. 'Forensics have completed a preliminary inspection of the drone fragments. They identified it as a Phantom Series Three, built by Chinese technology company DJI based in Shenzhen. We're tracking down local suppliers and checking purchase orders to see if we can come up with any leads.'

He cleared his throat and referred to his notes. 'As you know, the drone was heavily customised. Apart from carrying C4 explosives, it was fitted with a modified pistol barrel and mechanism capable of firing three nine millimetre rounds. Forensics suggest the C4 could've been rigged to either detonate remotely or on impact with its target. It had an effective blast radius of around eight metres, so we're fortunate it didn't get any closer than it did.' Pausing to sweep a glance over the assembled group, he dipped his head at them. 'Well done. Thanks to our efforts the premier is safe, and while he's cancelled his meeting at the council chambers, he's eager to go ahead with tonight's dinner function.' He caught Simpson's eye and nodded.

Simpson glanced around the table. 'Well that's it for the PTG today. After the meeting we'll be leaving the premier in your capable hands. Tomorrow morning we'll rendezvous here again to assist with the escort back to the airport. Of course we'll be on-call if needed.'

'Thank you, Mr Simpson, your unit's presence was appreciated today.' Sullivan addressed the group again. 'With Olman's private bodyguards, assistance from the local police and the addition of Mr Ryan and Mr Williams, I believe we will have ample security for tonight's proceedings.' He turned to Modeen. 'Now, Ms Bennet, what can you tell us about the individual you pursued along the Esplanade?'

Modeen took her time answering, choosing her words carefully. 'I was looking for anyone suspicious and he stood out in the crowd.'

'Stood out … how?'

'He was dark-skinned but struck me as being more African American than Indigenous Australian or Islander. And he was tall, approximately six-two, with a military hairstyle and carrying a bulky-looking back-pack. And when I made a move to intercept him, he started to run, which confirmed my suspicions.'

'I see. And you pursued him?'

'Yes, but during the pursuit, two hired thugs distracted me long enough for him to get away.'

'Distracted you, how?'

Not wanting to go into detail, Modeen replied curtly, 'They tried to detain me.'

Sullivan eyed her but left it at that. 'Where are they now?'

'In police custody, being checked over at the hospital.'

'Did you have a chance to question them?'

'Yes, and they gave me a name … Eli Washington. According to the man I questioned, Washington hired them from the Pussycat Club here in Cairns. Do you have any intel on that club?'

When Sullivan turned to Bellamy and raised his eyebrows, Bellamy flicked Modeen a belligerent glance and said sulkily, 'The Pussycat Club is one of three adult nightclubs in the city. It's one of the more reputable joints, we don't see much trouble there.' When he looked back at Sullivan, the chief prompted, 'Who runs it?'

This time Bellamy ignored Modeen, speaking directly to Sullivan.

'Until recently it had an international owner, one Akeem Jibril, but has since been taken over by an Aussie-based organisation.'

At the mention of Jibril, the former Spear of Allah 2IC and now deceased as a result of a previous NatSec mission, Modeen and Wolf shared a glance and shifted in their seats.

Modeen eyed Bellamy. 'And who heads this Aussie organisation?'

Bellamy continued to address his responses to Sullivan. 'Its ABN is listed as "The trustee for the Davidson Family Trust".'

'So,' Wolf barked, 'who is the trustee?'

'Not sure.' The furtive look that crossed Bellamy's face wasn't lost on Modeen, who felt a familiar prickle on the back of her neck. 'But I know the manager, sir,' he went on hurriedly to Sullivan, 'and I'll get him to follow that up with their accountant. Leave it with me.'

———

Spooky set up his laptop and tapped on an icon tagged 'Ben', while Modeen and Wolf looked on. The three were huddled around the small coffee table in Modeen's apartment when, a moment later, Ben's face appeared on the screen. He nodded a greeting and got straight down to business.

'Sit rep, team.'

He listened intently to Modeen's outline of the recent events, and then made a report of his own. 'I've gathered some further intel on Reger. His alias, Kyle Davidson, is the younger brother of William Davidson, who is registered as the trustee of the Davidson Family Trust. According to my source, Kyle was in Reger's army unit and *was* KIA, so Reger assumed his name. He and Jackson Foster obviously know William

Davidson through association, and my guess is all three have a vested interest in the Pussycat Club. It appears Davidson took control of the club only about a month before we raided Jibril's place at Port Douglas.'

Ben paused before going on, his voice low, his words clipped and concise. 'Our intel suggests the club has links with prostitution and, more recently, the supply of crystal meth, so it's of concern the police consider it one of the more reputable clubs in Cairns. The use of Ice among young adults in the city is reported to've tripled in the last two years, while in Brisbane, Sydney and Melbourne it's out of control. We've been ordered to assist the Feds in shutting down these operations where possible, so after you've secured Olman tonight, I want you to check out the Pussycat Club and see if you can chase up some leads.'

———

Jackson Foster held the mobile against his ear. Wincing and keeping his voice down, he said dully, 'The drone was destroyed before it could reach its target.'

A frustrated sigh reverberated from the other end of the call. 'You tried to get too creative ... I warned you about that. Just keep it simple and focus on Olman for now. Do you hear what I'm saying?'

Foster ran a hand over his face and muttered, 'Yeah, I hear.'

'Will you get another opportunity before he leaves Cairns?'

'It's gonna be harder now he's cancelled the rest of his appointments for the day … but there might be an opening tomorrow morning,' and Foster's expression lifted, 'to give him a decent send-off.' He gave an amused snort and then sobered. 'What about the others?'

'We'll deal with them *after* we've finished with Olman.' Not waiting for a response, Jon Reger ended the call.

———

'Did you see the way those local members sucked up to Olman?' Modeen murmured to Wolf at her side.

'Yeah,' Wolf drawled softly, pressing the button to summon the elevator, 'and the little prick revelled in every minute of it.'

'Well,' Modeen breathed, 'the night went without a hitch at least.' She yawned. 'I'm looking forward to leaving the premier to the safety of his presidential suite.'

'You and me both.'

When the lift doors swished open, they filed in and waited for Olman and his burly bodyguards to join them. With so many large people in it the elevator felt crowded. Cheesy canned music crackled from a corner speaker and a smell arose from the floor carpet Modeen didn't want to identify.

When it appeared nobody else was inclined to do so, she pushed her way forward and aggressively thumbed the button to get the lift moving.

Stepping back as the doors closed, she found herself sandwiched between Olman and one of his brawny bodyguards. To her dismay, Olman fixed his eyes on her.

He took his time looking her up and down, taking in her athletic and undeniably feminine physique, striking blue eyes and fine features, before announcing, 'I hear you were in the armed forces. I was a senior officer in the Army myself you know, *and* I saw active service.'

Feeling him press closer and brush a hand over her hip, she gave a shudder of revulsion. And when he leaned in to whisper, 'How about we share war stories over a nightcap?' and had the audacity to stroke her buttock, her reflexes kicked in and she thrust an elbow up and sideways, hard, cracking him square on the nose.

His head snapped back and rebounded against the lift's mirrored wall. With a grunt of pain he reeled forward, clutching his nose.

One of his bodyguards had instinctively reached for his shoulder holster, but froze on feeling the cold muzzle of Wolf's Glock press against his temple.

'We're all friends here,' Wolf drawled, as the lift doors opened.

Letting loose a string of expletives, Olman dragged out a handkerchief to soak up the blood pouring from his nose, blubbing, 'You broke my nose. You broke my *F'N* nose!'

'We'd better get that seen to.' While ushering Olman out of the lift, the second of his two bodyguards threw Modeen an approving half smile.

As they remained in the elevator, watching the two bodyguards assist the profanity-spitting premier into his apartment, Wolf holstered his Glock and turned to Modeen with a sly grin as the lift doors swished closed.

# CHAPTER EIGHT

At just before o-one hundred, the streets of inner city Cairns had emptied of vehicles save the occasional cruising taxi, to become the haunt of staggering nightclub patrons high on one substance or another, raucous tourists taking the party to the streets, and the odd drunken brawl.

When the hulking, stern-faced bouncer at the Pussycat Club opened the door to allow another patron to enter, doof-doof music thumped out into the street. Dressed in figure-hugging black pants and crimson silk blouse, Modeen slipped past him and into the dimly lit nightclub.

After pausing while her eyes adjusted to the low light, she began wading through the heaving sea of sweating bodies, slapping away the odd grabby hand as she went.

On centre stage a nubile woman wearing nothing

but a G-string gyrated her taut young body around a stainless steel pole. Strobe lights bounced off the ceiling as the mostly Gen Y patrons dry-humped on the dance floor or jostled two deep at the bar, yelling hoarsely to be heard over the pounding music.

The tribal pulse emitting from six huge speakers mounted around the room reverberated through to the core of each member of the jam-packed audience.

In a back corner, Spooky stepped into the light and caught Modeen's eye. He held up four fingers and then pointed toward the rear of the room. She glanced over and saw a man standing guard in front of a door, brawny arms crossed over a thick chest. His wide stance appeared fixed to that spot, from where he stared impassively at the swaying crowd.

When Modeen turned back, she glimpsed Wolf slide in through the front door. Before he was swallowed up in the crowd, she raised a hand to catch his eye. When their gazes met, she indicated the back of the room with a tilt of her head, the strobing blue light gleaming off her platinum blonde hair like a silver halo.

She frowned when her nose picked up the scent of booze and stale garlic as a hot breath puffed into her ear, 'What time d'ya go on stage, gorgeous?' The young, buck-toothed male wore a goofy leer as he eyed her up and down. Not bothering to hide her distaste, she shoved him aside and made her way to the back of the club.

The guard's expression remained impassive as he watched her push through the last of the crowd to stand in front of him. And when she glanced pointedly at the door handle, he merely stood fast and shook his head.

His expression changed abruptly when Modeen gave a shrug and then stepped in to thrust her knee into his groin. He gave a grunt of agony and was bending double when she followed up with an elbow under his chin, using her whole body weight to add momentum to the thrust.

His head reeled back and when he brought it forward again, his pained expression turned to one of fury as he fixed dark eyes on hers.

When she bestowed an innocent smile on him and stepped to the side, he frowned. Distracted, he had no time to react as Wolf burst through the crowd and came at him with a pile driving kick to the mid-section.

The force of the blow and the man's weight against it tore the door off its hinges. Like a surfer riding a wave, the guard rode the crashing, splintering door into what appeared to be a small hallway. Before he came to a sliding stop, Modeen and Wolf had stepped through the opening. The crowd, in the grip of the music's pounding throb, was oblivious to the commotion.

A door to their left opened suddenly and another bouncer entered the corridor. He propped on seeing them, and then made for her, the easier of the two targets … or so he thought. When he was within reaching distance, she faded to her left and then executed a side kick to his leading leg's knee cap.

With a sickening crack, his knee buckled sideways and his leg collapsed under his weight. As he crumpled, she followed through with a knee to his face. His head jerked back as he slumped to the floor, out cold.

When a third bouncer charged through the door, Modeen grabbed his arm as he reached for her. Using his momentum, she rolled her shoulders, bent her knees, and threw him across the hallway. Wolf leapt between them and as the bouncer tried to get back up, knocked him out with a right cross to the side of the face.

Behind them, Spooky pulled the Glock from his shoulder holster as he entered the hallway and covered them as they went through the connecting doorway.

In the next room, a heavily-built man sat at an impressive double pedestal mahogany desk with a laptop and leather-bound ledger open in front of him. The room was dimly lit and had an impressive floor-to-ceiling bookshelf running the length of the wall behind the desk. Leather reclining chairs were set-up around the room, and a huge flat screen TV hung from the wall behind them.

Another man in a loose-fitting double-breasted suit, obviously a bodyguard, stood fast at the end of the desk.

When Modeen and Wolf entered the room, the man

behind the desk slammed the ledger and laptop closed and fixed them with a challenging gaze as they halted in front of him.

The bodyguard reacted by pulling a nine millimetre Ruger pistol from the shoulder holster beneath his suit coat and stepping forward. When he levelled it at Modeen's forehead she slapped both hands around the weapon and, in one fluid motion, removed the gun from his grip to point it back at him. He was left staring, dumbfounded, at his empty hand.

The man behind the desk slumped back in his seat with a roll of eyes at the guard.

Satisfied the situation was under control, Spooky pulled the door closed and took up sentry duty in the hallway. From there, the music in the nightclub was a more bearable dull rhythmic thump.

The man behind the desk eyed the two intruders belligerently and growled, 'Hope you got a warrant.'

Modeen smiled. 'We don't need warrants.'

That gave him pause. After a few moments, he said more civilly, 'You federal police?'

Modeen continued to smile. 'All you need to know is that we're authorised to use deadly force if necessary.' Holding up her phone to show him a picture of Jackson Foster, she said sweetly, 'Now, what can you tell us about this man?'

Flicking a passing glance at the photo, the man said flatly as though reading from a script, 'Never seen him before.'

Wolf had circled around the desk and was checking the drawers. He lifted a silver Smith and Wesson thirty-eight Snub-nosed Special from the centre compartment, showed it to Modeen, and then tucked it into the front waistband of his dark blue jeans.

'Interesting thing to find in a desk drawer. Mine just has pens and paperclips.' Modeen's smile evaporated and she barked, 'Who are you?'

When the man sneered, 'You find out,' Wolf grabbed him by the back of the head and slammed his face against the desk.

Blood spurted from the man's nose as he raised his contorted face, clamping both hands tightly around his nose.

Spying the jacket draped over the back of the man's chair, Wolf proceeded to rifle through it.

When the man saw him pull out a bulging wallet, he spat, 'That's *mine,*' and frothy saliva mixed with the blood on his face.

Wolf merely raised an eyebrow at him while removing the driver's licence and flicking it like a Frisbee onto the desk in front of Modeen.

'You're not being very smart *or* very cooperative,' Modeen said, picking up the licence and inspecting it. It read *William Nathan Davidson.*

Behind the desk Wolf frisked the bodyguard. Removing a flick knife from the man's back pocket and then pushing him into a chair, he ripped a cord from the desk lamp and bound the man's hands behind his back.

Tossing the licence back onto the desk, Modeen pointed the bodyguard's gun at Davidson. 'Get up, you're taking us on a tour of the premises.'

Seeing Wolf collect the laptop from off the desk and use his smart phone to photograph entries in the ledger, Davidson yelled over his shoulder, 'You won't find anything. I'm clean.'

Muttering, 'That's highly unlikely,' Modeen ushered him to the door.

As it opened, Spooky moved aside and kept his gun at the ready, trained on the other three bouncers grouped at the end of the corridor. The doof-doof thump of music intensified as they made their way along the hallway. The bouncers sat with their backs against the wall and heads bowed, looking sorry for themselves. Two of them glanced up as Davidson was pushed past them, and were rewarded with dark glowers as he stepped over the door still lying on the floor.

'Where's the storeroom?' Modeen yelled over the music's increasing volume.

Davidson shrugged. 'Huh?'

As she pushed him forward, a crack of light appeared in the wall near the end of the bar and a barman emerged through a concealed doorway, carrying an armful of bourbon bottles. With a frustrated sigh, Davidson dropped his chin to his chest, shaking his head. Modeen grinned and nudged him toward the concealed doorway.

The storeroom was the same size as Davidson's office. It was stacked to the ceiling with kegs of beer and cartons of wine and spirits. A double roller door took up most of the rear wall and provided easy access from outside.

When Wolf finished checking the room over, he came to stand next to Modeen.

Davidson lifted his chin and muttered, 'This is all there is. There's nothing else to see.' His expression grew mutinous. 'And I wanna know who's gonna pay for the damage to my door.'

'Don't worry,' Modeen said sweetly, 'we'll be back to talk to you again soon.'

Seeing Wolf still holding his laptop, Davidson reached for it, exclaiming, 'I'll take that.' He was rewarded with a hard shove to the chest from the heel of Wolf's palm. It sent him to the floor on one knee, gasping for breath.

They left him moaning on the storeroom floor and collected Spooky on their way out. The bouncer positioned outside the nightclub's front door was oblivious to goings-on inside, and barely glanced at the three as they passed him to stroll nonchalantly down Spence Street toward the Esplanade.

• • •

Back in Modeen's apartment at the Pullman International, Spooky and Wolf pulled up chairs to the circular table near the sliding door. After ensuring the drapes were tightly closed, Modeen peered over their shoulders to see Spooky checking files on the laptop, while Wolf scanned the photos he had taken of Davidson's ledger entries.

With a muttered, 'Pretty much standard for what you'd expect from a nightclub,' he leaned back in his chair and stretched while passing his phone to Modeen. 'We're in the wrong business. Check out how much those pole dancers make per shift.'

Spooky raised his eyes from the computer screen. 'How much?'

The corner of Wolf's lips tipped into a teasing grin. 'More than your mother ever got paid.'

'My mother was never a pole dancer!'

'Oh alright, exotic dancer then.' Wolf winked at a grinning Modeen.

Spooky rolled his eyes. *Whatever.*

Handing him the phone, Modeen murmured, 'And it doesn't look like that includes tips, Spook.' After giving him a moment to read the screen and shake his head in disbelief at the large figure captured in the camera shot, she said matter-of-factly, 'Have you found anything interesting on the laptop?'

Still staring at the phone, he muttered, 'Nothing stands out yet.' He glanced up at her. 'There are some references to a few properties … a brothel in Earlville, a place in East Trinity, and a cattle station out west at Julia Creek.'

'Where the hell is Julia Creek?' Wolf piped up.

'About six hundred and fifty kilometres west of Townsville.' Seeing his blank look, Modeen added, 'You know, on the way to Mt Isa?'

'Oh right.' He glanced across at Spooky, who responded with raised eyebrows and a shrug.

Thrusting both hands on her hips, Modeen exclaimed, *'Really?* Haven't you guys ever been out west?'

Putting down the phone, Spooky turned his attention to the computer screen again. 'Meth labs vent a lot of toxic gas and smoke, so if they're into making Ice, I can't see them doing it at a club in the middle of the CBD. They'd need a super heavy duty extraction and ventilation system.'

Modeen sucked on her bottom lip. 'Yeah, the club looked pretty clean.' She pulled up a chair and Wolf made room for her to join them at the table. 'They could be selling the stuff from the club, but I doubt they'd situate a drug lab there, it's too obvious a location. If there is a lab, it's more likely to be in a remote place like Julia Creek, out of sight and away from everything.' She sat forward. 'East Trinity's about forty-five minutes south of here. After we see Olman safely off, I reckon we should head there and check out Davidson's property.'

# CHAPTER NINE

The following morning Modeen and Spooky waited outside the presidential suite as the premier and his entourage of PAs and minders prepared to make their way to the airport for the journey back to Brisbane. Stepping into the hallway and seeing Modeen, Olman glared at her and stuck out his chin.

As they drew nearer he snarled at her, 'I've had words with your superiors. You're in big trouble, lady.'

Her eyebrow twitched on seeing the purple smudges under his eyes and the visible bruising beneath the plaster covering the bridge of his nose, and she swallowed a grin.

Noticing her struggle to keep a straight face, his eyes narrowed menacingly and his lips compressed into a tight line. Tugging his already straight suit coat even straighter, he stalked past with his plastered nose in the air.

Wolf was waiting for them on the front steps of the hotel with Kevin Simpson of the PTG. The two men stood quietly, their focus on the job at hand. Council workers had set up barricades at each end of the street in preparation for the premier's departure.

The government 7-series BMW sedan, led by two police motorcycles and backed up by two armoured TPG Toyota Landcruisers, pulled smoothly into the colonnade with a squeak of tyres on polished tiles. As soon as the BMW came to a stop, Wolf moved to check it over while Simpson, dressed in black fatigues, bullet-proof vest and helmet, stood guard armed with a Heckler and Koch MP5 machine gun.

Satisfied all was clear, Wolf nodded at Simpson, who ushered the premier's entourage forward.

Tightly flanked by his bodyguards, Olman was hurried down the hotel's front steps and into the waiting BMW. Modeen and Spooky took up sentry on opposite sides of the colonnade and waited for Simpson and Wolf to jump into the first of the imposing black Landcruisers.

They followed suit into the second and had just enough time to fasten their seatbelts before the procession of vehicles began to pull away from the hotel.

In the back of the Landcruiser, Modeen's mobile chimed and she put it to her ear. 'Hey Ben.'

'JD. How are things progressing?'

'We're enroute to the airport with the premier.'

'Good. By the way, we've received a formal complaint from the premier's office.'

'Oh yeah?'

'They're claiming you assaulted him. So what happened?'

Modeen gave a snort. 'Sexual harassment is what happened.'

'Jack wants details so he can make a formal response.' At the mention of Jack Pender, NatSec's Operations Manager, Modeen sobered.

'The premier felt it was within his rights to make an improper suggestion to me. And when he groped me in front of witnesses in a crowded lift, I simply gave him the appropriate response.'

Ben sighed. 'Yeah … I thought it'd be something like that.' He paused and then said, 'Leave it with me. But next time try not to leave obvious bruises, JD. Just break a coupl'a fingers or something. Pollies are precious about their faces, and this little man's vainer than most.'

Her lips twitched. 'Point taken, Ben.'

There was a thread of amusement in his deep voice when he said, 'Consider yourself disciplined,' and rung off.

Ahead of the convoy, the road barricades were removed and they progressed along Abbott Street to merge with the Esplanade and follow the city's foreshore north. Skirting around the Northern Reserve

Sports Grounds they negotiated a roundabout and turned right into Lake Street.

Thickly foliaged trees lined the road to provide shade for cars and spectators watching the soccer and hockey games, but at ten o'clock that morning, the sports ground was deserted.

In the air-conditioned BMW, Olman gingerly fingered the plaster across his nose and muttered sourly to no one in particular, 'I'll be glad to see the last of this dump.' Out of the corner of his eye he noticed a sudden bright flash and whipped his head around.

His eyes widened in fear at the same time as the driver let out a blood-curdling shriek.

A rocket-propelled grenade hurtled across the open paddock toward them.

It slammed into the front quarter panel just behind the driver's side wheel arch, throwing the vehicle off the ground and hurling it sideways. It tumbled over and over in a fireball of smoke and flame.

The Landcruisers following screeched to a sliding halt on the street behind. An officer from the first vehicle leapt out carrying a small fire extinguisher. He raced to the downed BMW and tried to extinguish the flames.

In the passenger seat of the second vehicle, Spooky yelled, 'There!' and pointed to thickets beyond the field, where a trail of smoke gave away the location of the rocket's origin.

He hit the startled driver on the arm. 'Go! *Go!* Over there!'

Throwing the Landcruiser into gear the driver accelerated hard, veered the big wagon to the right, jumped the kerb and smashed through the bollards separating the road from the sports field. In the back seat, Modeen braced herself, trying to get a clear view ahead. The driver floored the accelerator and the V8 responded with a throaty roar. He fought to control the speeding vehicle as it fish-tailed across the rain-slicked oval.

Ahead of them, Foster catapulted out of the thickets on a green Kawasaki KLR trail bike, a rooster tail of dirt spraying from the rear wheel of the six hundred CC machine. He skirted around the back of the sports ground as the black Landcruiser altered course across the field in a bid to cut him off.

Leaving the officer with the extinguisher and the motorcycle policemen to deal with the shattered and smoking BMW, the other Landcruiser joined the chase. Smoke poured from its rear wheels as the driver threw the vehicle into reverse and it careered backwards.

Wolf gripped the handle above the window, his knuckles whitening as the vehicle spun one-eighty degrees and then took off at speed back down Lake Street.

Beside the driver, Simpson yelled, 'Cut him off! Take the next left!' Grabbing the police radio handset, he jammed a finger on the Transmit button and barked,

'Ambulance required on Lake Street, between Rutherford and Lily. Vehicle rollover, possibly four casualties, one VIP.'

In the other Landcruiser, Modeen and Spooky had taken their pistols from their holsters. They buzzed down their windows preparing to take a shot, but the bike passed too quickly and the heavy Toyota drifted right, its all-terrain tyres throwing up clumps of soft ground. Then, as Foster once more sped across their path, Modeen saw an opportunity and fired off two quick rounds.

They fell in behind the trail bike and watched as it wavered and then jerked, its engine coughing as flames erupted from its fuel tank. With fire licking at his legs, Foster tried to exit the southern end of the field. The big bike surged forward one last time before its motor abruptly stalled. Slamming on the back brake, Foster laid the bike down. As it slid to a halt, rear wheel spinning uselessly in the air, he leapt off, stumbling and trying to stay on his feet. Rapidly patting out the flames on his jeans, he raced across Lily Street toward the Harbour City Views apartment complex. Taking a gigantic leap, he grabbed the top of the high security gate, vaulted over it, and disappeared down the driveway.

'Suspect is in the grounds of the Harbour City apartments,' Modeen called over the comms as their vehicle skidded to a halt outside the northern end of the complex. Spooky leapt from the passenger seat and raced to the fence with Modeen right behind him. They vaulted the gate in unison.

When the other Landcruiser screeched to a halt at the apartments' southern end, Wolf and Simpson sprang out. They scaled the fence and ran into the complex while the driver took up arms and remained by the vehicle. Wolf sprinted ahead of Simpson, who was weighed down by his restrictive tactical gear.

The complex's labyrinth of apartment blocks, narrow driveways and garages made it difficult to cover all access routes and thoroughfares. Wolf glanced behind at Simpson and pointed to the left before veering right. Simpson nodded and went left. Ahead of them at the northern end, Modeen and Spooky had also peeled off. The team moved cautiously, checking ahead of themselves at each turn.

At the short, harsh burst of a machine gun close by, they all pressed themselves against the nearest wall and listened. When another sharp burst rang out from in front and to the right of her, Modeen raced around the corner, her Walther PPQ at the ready.

She slid to a stop at the sight of Foster standing over Simpson who was sprawled on the ground. Foster bent lower to hold the muzzle of Simpson's MP5 a mere inch above the prostrate man's forehead.

Modeen sprinted toward them and shouted, 'HEY!'

Whipping his head around, Foster took a step back to level the gun at her, but she was already on him. Using his leading leg as a step, she 'ran' up the front of him, bringing a knee forward as she did so and punching it, hard and sharp, into his face.

His head snapped back and the gun fell from his hands as he collapsed backward in a heap. Modeen 'rode' him to the ground and executed a forward roll behind him. Rolling smoothly to her feet, she came up with Walt in both hands.

Keeping the pistol trained on Foster, she moved forward to check on Simpson, who lay groaning and clutching the front of his bulletproof vest. An instant later Wolf and Spooky raced around the corner. They propped on seeing Foster face-up and unconscious with Modeen covering him from a short distance away.

As they approached she glanced at them and inclined her head at Simpson. 'He's been hit.'

Gasping, 'I'll live,' Simpson sat up with a grimace.

While Spooky helped him to his feet, Wolf lifted a set of handcuffs from Simpson's vest. He rolled Foster over, checked for a pulse, and cuffed his hands behind his back, drawling, 'So will he.'

Modeen lowered her pistol but kept it by her side and her eyes on Foster while the other two examined Simpson's vest. At the peppering of bullet holes in the front of it, Spooky threw Wolf a meaningful glance and began ripping open the Velcro straps.

As they peeled off the vest and dropped it to the ground, Simpson gave a wince of pain and doubled over, clutching his chest.

Putting away her pistol, Modeen said, 'You guys

grab Foster. I'll help Simpson back to the car.' Moving to Simpson's side, she lent him a shoulder and they made their way slowly to the waiting Landcruiser.

The other two grabbed one of Foster's arms each and dragged him toward the vehicle, the limp toes of his jackboots scraping the paving as they went. At their approach, the officer standing guard by the car hurried forward to assist Modeen with Simpson.

Foster began to come around, shaking his head in an attempt to clear it while saying nothing, merely glaring darkly at them. They pushed him against the side of the car and Wolf kept a hand on his throat while Spooky climbed into the back seat. Then Wolf shoved Foster in beside Spooky and got in himself, wedging their captive between them.

'I'll meet you back at the Beamer.' Modeen had to raise her voice over the approaching shriek of sirens as police and emergency service vehicles sped to the scene of the accident.

Closing the car door, she tapped the roof twice and then took off at a fast jog back to the northern entrance of the complex. By the time she met the others back at the wrecked BMW, paramedics were busy attending to the injured, including Simpson.

Seeing her, Spooky strode to her side. 'Olman's minders survived relatively unscathed, but the driver didn't make it.' He indicated a tarp-covered form lying on the roadside.

Modeen frowned. 'What about Olman?'

'Fractured arm and a coupl'a broken ribs.' He raised a mocking eyebrow. 'Apparently politicians of his stature aren't required to wear seatbelts, something I'm sure the Police would be interested to hear.'

With a derisive snort and a sideways glance at the ambulance, he went on. 'They're taking him to the Cairns private hospital for observation.'

Modeen nodded and murmured, 'Wolf get anything out of Foster?'

'Nah, he didn't say a word. But Wolf lifted this off him on the way here.' Pulling a mobile phone part way out of the pocket of his cargo pants, Spooky slid it back inside once Modeen had caught a glimpse.

'Good.' She nodded again. 'I'll get him to stay with Foster, although I doubt the Feds will let us interrogate him first, considering this is their operation.' She paused, thoughtful. 'I don't think this is over … I'd better speak to Sullivan and make sure they put a guard on the premier's hospital room. Then we'll head back to the hotel and see if we can get any contact details off that phone.'

Spooky eyed her. 'That's not going to be easy. I had a quick look and we're gonna have to crack the password on it first.'

When she dipped her head in acknowledgement and went to move off, he said, 'Before we go, check this out.' He led her to one of the waiting Landcruisers and opened the rear door. 'This look familiar?'

Modeen peered down at the rocket launcher Foster

had used. 'An RPG 7 … fitted with a PGO telescopic sight … like the ones the Iraqi Army use.' She raised her head to meet Spooky's gaze. 'Why would they go to all the trouble of bringing one of these into the country?'

As more official-looking cars arrived to surround the scene, Spooky stepped back and closed the door. Turning to Modeen, he murmured, 'That's what worries me. These guys are using some serious weaponry. As you know, those seven series BMWs are armoured and pretty tough, but the grenade ripped right into it. It must've had a dual HEAT warhead to cause that sort of damage.'

Before moving off, he leaned in closer to say, 'I'll tell Wolf to stay with Foster, and let Simpson know we're taking the other PTG vehicle back to the hotel.'

———

Back at Spooky's apartment in the Pullman, he and Modeen sat in the small lounge room with the mobile phone Wolf had taken from Foster on the coffee table in front of them. Spooky was busy pulling the back cover off it.

When Modeen asked, 'What type of phone is it?' he studied the inside of the cover and muttered, 'Nokia Lumia, six-two-five.'

'Take out the SIM.' As she spoke, Modeen opened

Spooky's laptop and placed it on the table between them.

When he handed her the Micro-SIM card, she pushed it into a small slot on the side of the computer, and then tapped on the keyboard, bringing up a decoder screen.

At the drop-down menu on the first window, she selected the six-two-five Nokia model. When a four and six digit code prompt appeared on the screen, she entered zeros into each space and clicked on the RESET button. The computer beeped and a message appeared on screen.

*Code reset successful.*

Pulling the SIM out of the computer, she handed it back to Spooky. 'Try now.'

Returning the card to its slot on the mobile and refitting the back cover, he turned the phone over and pressed the ON button.

When, twelve seconds later, a Nokia password screen appeared, he entered four zeros and waited as the phone cycled through its start-up. When it prompted for the Windows password, he entered another six zeros and then swiped the Welcome screen upward.

Modeen leaned in closer as he scrolled slowly through the Recent Calls log. One number stood out as having multiple Sent and Received calls logged.

Sitting back, Modeen muttered, 'Ten to one, that's Reger's number.'

At a sharp rap on the door Spooky rose and let Wolf into the apartment, while Modeen continued checking through the messages on Foster's phone.

As he strode into the room Wolf announced, 'The Feds took Foster to their HQ. They think he was working alone.' Taking the Glock from his shoulder holster, he pulled back the slide, caught the ejected nine millimetre cartridge, and then thumbed the unused bullet back into the clip, all while continuing with his report.

'Olman's been admitted, he'll be in the Cairns private hospital overnight. There are two federal agents posted outside his door and one of his minders in the room with him at all times. Simpson's been taken to Cairns Base Hospital for x-rays. They're keeping him in there overnight for observation.' He took a seat beside Modeen. 'How'd you go with the phone?'

'Good job lifting it.' Modeen glanced at him with a smile as Spooky resumed his seat opposite them. 'Nicely done.'

Wolf grinned back at her. 'Ta.'

She passed him the mobile. 'There's one number that's a real stand-out. Foster made several calls to it and received a number from it over the last few days. We assume it's Reger's mobile. There's also a text message from someone calling himself 'Ogata' but there was nothing in the message field. Ben's checking out the number and the name to see if he can come up with anything on either of them. Apart from that, it hasn't given us much else. It appears Foster wasn't big on texting and didn't receive many texts either.'

Wolf lifted his eyes from studying the phone's screen. 'So, what's our plan of attack?'

'Well...,' and she sat back to glance thoughtfully at the ceiling. 'I guess with Olman secure, and while we're waiting for more intel from Ben, we could check out Davidson's place at East Trinity.'

Spooky slapped his hands together. 'Sounds good to me.'

'Yeah,' Wolf drawled, 'and with Sullivan and the rest of the Feds busy with Foster, he won't be going anywhere anytime soon. We've got some wriggle room.' He handed the phone back to Modeen. She was about to get up from the table when Spooky's NatSec mobile buzzed. He took it out, glanced at the screen and then at the others.

'It's Ben.' Putting the phone in the centre of the table, he pressed a button and said, 'Go ahead, Ben, I have you on speaker. Modeen and Wolf are here with me.'

'I've been in touch with Sullivan and he's filled me in on events. I'm heading to Cairns to coordinate with the Feds and help with Foster's interrogation. I want you to check out the East Trinity property on your way south to Townsville.'

'Townsville?'

'Yeah, Spook. I've organised a Taipan from the 5$^{th}$ Aviation Regiment to pick you up at o-one hundred hours from Townsville RAAF base. They'll brief you in the air, but needless to say, you'll be conducting a covert assault on the cattle station at Julia Creek. Satellite photos reveal heavily guarded buildings, and the heat signatures coming from the central barn are impressive, to say the least.'

Spooky shuffled forward in his seat and was about to speak when Ben went on. 'In case you're wondering … Spook … sending in a drone is not an option in this situation.' Spooky's shoulders slumped as Ben continued. 'We want to avoid collateral damage if possible. However, the Taipan will remain in the area should you need air support.'

'What sort of numbers are we up against, and are they run-of-the-mill thugs or trained mercenaries?'

'I'm not sure how many are ex-army like Reger and Foster, JD, but from the satellite images it appears there are twenty people on site. I'm guessing at least eight would be general hands and lab workers. The others will probably be a mix of military personnel and members of the "Black Mamba" gang. So it looks like Reger and Foster have forged some new alliances.'

Modeen frowned. 'Black Mamba? Are these guys from South Africa?'

'No, they're a New Zealand gang of predominately Maori and Pacific Islander members. Apparently the gang leader has a fascination with black mamba snakes. So much so, it's reported he even had the inside of his lips and mouth tattooed black. Anyway, since Olman's legislation outlawed motorcycle gangs, Black Mamba has moved into what was Hells Angels territory on the Gold Coast. Because they weren't named in the Queensland anti-gang laws, they've managed to dodge the state-wide crackdown.'

'That's crazy.'

Ben gave a snort. 'I know that's how it sounds, Wolf, but in fact it's just legislation and politics, neither of which make sense a lot of the time. Because Black Mamba members as a rule don't ride bikes, they aren't considered a motorcycle gang, which means the police can't arrest them for simply hanging out together like they can with other bikers. Although the exodus of other gangs from Queensland might seem like good news, in reality they've simply relocated south to NSW and Victoria where those laws don't exist.'

Modeen leaned forward in her seat. 'That explains the large, dark-skinned bouncers we keep running into.'

'Yes. And I believe the name Ogata on the text Foster received is a reference to a Japanese chemist, one Akira Ogata, who was the first to synthesize crystal meth back in nineteen-nineteen. I think Ogata is a code name for a crystal meth operation at Julia Creek.' Ben paused before saying grimly, 'Black Mamba are hard core, into serious violence, firearms and drug distribution. They're also actively recruiting to swell their ranks. Don't underestimate these guys. Dylan did and look what happened to him. I don't want the same thing happening to any of you.'

―――――

Thirty-two minutes south of the town of Ayr on the Bruce Highway, a convoy of four black late model Ford sedans slowed to a crawl. All four vehicles were riding low, their suspension compressed by the weight of their male occupants and boots full of assorted firearms.

The two rear vehicles indicated and turned left onto the Woodstock to Giru Road, which would take them west through Charters Towers and on to Richmond and their final destination, Julia Creek.

Back on the Bruce Highway, the two lead vehicles continued toward the sprawling city of Townsville. Having taken the ring road that skirted the city, the two black sedans motored northward.

Three hours later, they passed the Warner Road turn-off just south of Cairns. Entering the city's outer suburbs, they cruised down Ray Jones Drive and turned into Sheridan Street in the heart of the Cairns CBD.

The tailing vehicle turned right and parked at the rear of the Cairns Private Hospital, while the lead vehicle continued north and pulled into the car park at the Federal Police building.

———

Modeen, Wolf and Spooky left the TPG Landcruiser parked at the Pullman. After checking out of the hotel, they piled into Modeen's hired M3 BMW sedan and headed south toward Gordonvale. The sedan's finely-tuned motor responded eagerly as Modeen accelerated through the gears, and the car slipped smoothly through the humid air and over the steaming bitumen.

Leaving the highway, they turned left into Warner Road and followed it through the row upon row of green cane pastures surrounding Green Hill. The cane pastures gave way to lush bushland as the road snaked its way along the increasingly hilly coastline.

Spooky glanced down at the GPS app on his

mobile. 'Turn left here. The house should be about fifty metres down that driveway,' and he pointed to an ostentatious wrought iron security gate.

Modeen pulled the BMW to the side of the road about twenty metres back from the entrance.

The single sliding gate was suspended between two imposing white pillars, and a heavy slab of hardwood engraved with *Haven on Trinity* sat atop them, completing the impressive façade. A tall white brick fence extended from both sides of the pillars, separated at regular intervals with panels of the same wrought iron pattern as the gate.

The white wall was obscured here and there by palm trees and stands of other thick tropical growth, but it appeared to encompass the estate's perimeter.

Spooky brought up a satellite image of the area on his phone and zoomed in on the house. 'Wow, check it out.' Leaning forward from the back seat, he held the phone between Wolf and Modeen so they could see. 'I reckon Hugh Heffner'd be happy owning this place. It's got two swimming pools, one on each deck. And check out that boat ramp.'

'Yeah, but why build something like this here, in East Trinity?' Glancing at the image, Wolf screwed up his nose. 'Isn't it a bit far from Cairns?'

Modeen stared thoughtfully at the phone's screen. 'I think that's the whole point. It's away from the city, but within easy reach of it. The old adage "out of sight is out of mind" would apply here, I reckon.'

Spooky pointed at the gates. 'Looks like there's a keypad and security cameras. Should we knock, or simply let ourselves in?'

'Let's give Mr Davidson the benefit of the doubt.' Modeen put the purring BMW into gear and nudged it up to the gate. Winding down the driver's side window, she pressed the call button on the keypad.

A responding loud buzz pulsated for ten seconds.

In the back seat, Spooky growled, 'Right, they've had their chance.'

Modeen raised a hand and said calmly, 'Waait….'

When the buzz continued for another ten seconds, she killed the motor and turned to Spooky. 'You slip down the side and try to work your way around to the front. Wolf and I'll head down the driveway.' She thumbed the boot release and got out of the car.

Spooky had already disappeared into the thick undergrowth as she made her way to the boot. Reaching into it, she opened her custom aluminium case, removed a pocket-sized monocular spy telescope and small black pouch, and shoved both into her back pocket. She glanced over at Wolf, who was studying the nearest section of fence.

At her approach, he took a wide stance. Bending his knees, he lowered his hands and gave her a nod. After a quick glance to measure the height, she skipped toward him and then leapt into the air. Catching her leading foot in his cupped hands, he boosted her to the top of the wall. As she slid down the other side, Wolf scaled the fence, using the wrought iron panel as a ladder of sorts. His movements were surprisingly lithe for a big man. Dropping to his feet on the other side of the wall next to Modeen, he raised a hand to indicate he'd go left.

Keeping low, they made their way down both sides of the tree-lined cobblestone driveway. The green canopy above their heads brought relief from the searing northern sun, but the tropical humidity soon had their clothes damp and clingy with sweat.

As the mansion came into view, Modeen crossed to the other side of the driveway and took refuge in the thick undergrowth next to Wolf. From that angle, the house looked like a single storey cottage with a double garage off to one side. Pulling out her spy scope she studied the building, checking each window and the roofline for signs of movement.

At her whispered, 'Looks clear,' Wolf lifted the Glock from his shoulder holster. Pulling back and releasing the slide, he murmured, 'I'll cover you.'

With a quick glance behind, she sprang forward like an Olympic runner on the starting blocks and sprinted across the oval carpark to the front entrance of the house.


At the Eastern edge of the estate, Spooky found himself walking in sand. He'd reached the point where the fence petered out as the property's boundary met the sandy shoreline at the head of Trinity Inlet. Wiping his face on his shirtsleeves, he felt more sweat run down his back beneath his shirt and exhaled through pursed lips. *Damn it's humid.*

Dropping to a squat, he stared up at the wall of floor-to-ceiling windows dominating the ocean side of the mansion's three levels. The infinity pools set into the massive second and third level entertainment decks glinted temptingly at him. He licked his lips at the thought of a cool dip and a cold drink and shook his head in awe.

Thinking, *this joint wouldn't look out of place among the mansions of the rich and famous on Sydney's foreshore,* he took another quick glance around.

*But where is everybody? The place looks deserted.*

He caught a hint of coral spawn on the salt-laden air, and could hear the cloudy water of the inlet lapping greasily against the hundred metre long jetty nearby. Its boat mooring was empty, making the structure look unwanted and forlorn. Across the inlet the hills were shrouded in heavy grey clouds, occasional tendrils of which clung to folds in the lush green terrain.

A low drone from nearby mangroves had him slapping his neck. Squashing the body of an opportunistic mosquito scout between his fingers, he flicked it away as more of the parasitic, disease-carrying insects arrived to hum around his ears. Taking his Glock from its holster and keeping his head down, he sprinted up the pathway twisting through the trees toward the mansion.

It led him to the rear of the building's lowest level. Pressing himself against the wall beside a large window, he twisted his head around to see inside but the tinted glass made it difficult to get a good look. Twisting back, he swept a glance over the grounds. There wasn't a maintenance worker, gardener, or being of any sort within cooee.

Moving from his spot, he crept along the wall until he came across a side door. It was made of solid hard-wood but with clear glass panel inserts. Through the panels he could see a roomy internal laundry. Giving the handle the obligatory wiggle, he wasn't surprised to find it locked. Raising the Glock, he was about to use the butt to smash the bottom glass quarter panel when he spied the faint green flash of a motion detector in the top corner of the room.

*Damn.*

———

When the sliding glass entrance doors of the Cairns Private Hospital swished open, the two women manning the main reception desk kept their eyes fixed on their computer screens. With all the busy hospital's comings and goings, neck strain was a definite possi-bility if they looked up every time the door opened.

At the sound of heavy footsteps squeaking across

the highly polished tiles and coming to a stop in front of the desk, one of the women raised her head, a well-rehearsed greeting on her tongue for this latest bunch of visitors. But when her eyes met the self-assured gaze of three brawny, menacing-looking Islanders, she stiffened.

The other woman heard her colleagues' intake of breath and glanced up, as the man standing closest to the counter placed both hands on it and leaned forward, splaying his beefy fingers. While over six foot tall himself, he was the smallest of the three. Swirly lines of a tribal tattoo covered the left side of his face and extended down his thick neck and shoulder. The letters B L A C K were tattooed in bold ink on the fingers of his right hand just below the knuckles, and M A M B A on the left.

He smiled at the receptionist and enquired pleasantly in a deep, gravelly voice, 'What room is Nigel Olman in?'

'Premier Olman? Oh … um….' The slightly flustered receptionist looked down at the patient list. 'Ward B on the second floor of the southern wing, in private room fourteen.' She looked up again, her brow creased. 'But I don't believe he's seeing visitors today.'

When the man's smile widened, revealing startlingly white teeth, she took an involuntary step back.

'That's alright, love,' he said smoothly, tapping a nonchalant finger on the desk. 'He'll make time for us, we're old friends.' Throwing her a wink, he turned and followed his companions to the elevator.

The other receptionist stared at the departing men through narrowed eyes. Moving closer to her workmate, she leaned in to murmur, 'Should we let them know they're about to have visitors?'

Her colleague frowned thoughtfully and then raised one eyebrow. 'Nah … that prima donna Olman gets enough special treatment. Anyway, there's an armed guard on the door and one inside the room.' She waved a dismissive hand. 'They'll be fine.'

The elevator doors opened on the second floor and the three men stepped out. They glanced both ways along the corridor and then fixed their eyes on the ward sister's desk nearby, where a pretty young nurse was being chatted up by a spiky-haired orderly.

Keeping his eyes on the amorous pair who didn't even glance their way, the smaller man, obviously the leader, indicated an arrow on the wall near the desk. It pointed left with the room numbers one to eighteen beneath it, while the numbers nineteen to thirty-six were displayed under an arrow pointing right.

The three men headed left, counting down the room numbers as they strode along the corridor, their black Doc Marten boots squeaking on the scrubbed floor. They passed and were passed by scurrying nursing staff and orderlies, most of whom ignored the men.

Those who did glance at the group gave them a wide berth.

They stopped at a T junction in the corridor. On the wall facing them another set of arrows pointed to rooms four to nine on the left and ten to fifteen on the right.

After checking first if anyone was watching, the leader of the trio lifted the front of his shirt and pulled a ten inch knife and sheath from the front waistband of his black parachute pants. He unclipped the strap that held the weapon in the sheath and then returned the sheath to his waist band, behind his back this time. Glancing sideways at his companions, he threw them a curt nod before setting off to the right with a purposeful stride.

The federal security guard standing in front of room fourteen yawned while rocking back and forth on his heels and toes, trying to get the blood circulating in his legs and feet. Standing for hours on end was a killer for the circulation. On hearing a heavy tread approaching down the corridor, he paused in his calisthenics and looked toward the sound. When the islander came around the corner, the guard stiffened and eyeballed him, taking in his size and general air of menace.

And when two more, even larger men followed the first, the guard reached a precautionary hand inside his suit coat. Before he could grasp his weapon, the lead man sprang forward with surprising agility and intercepted his hand, at the same time using his free fist to slam the guard in the side of the head, sending him crashing against the door frame.

Inside the room Premier Olman scowled and thumped the bed with his good arm, muttering peevishly, 'How's a person supposed to get any rest with all the noise around here? If it's not alarms going off at all hours, it's people thumping around outside and banging gurneys into walls.'

His personal guard didn't answer, but lowered the newspaper he'd been reading to frown at the door.

In the corridor, the stunned guard rebounded off the wall and his attacker grabbed the lapels of his suit coat to swing him around and into the arms of his two grinning companions. After first relieving him of his Glock, they took turns pounding the guard with burly, tattooed fists. When he doubled over in pain, they picked up his body between them and used it as a battering ram, smashing down the door to room fourteen.

As the door burst inward and off its hinges, Olman sat bolt upright. At the same time his personal guard threw down the newspaper and leapt to his feet, gazing in disbelief at the federal guard lying contorted and bleeding on top of the ruined door, his neck twisted at an unnatural angle.

A moment later the first of the islanders entered the room, the dead guard's Glock in his hand. He levelled the gun at Olman's personal guard, who reacted instantly by kicking the pistol out of the man's hand.

Following up with a combination left and right hook, and then a driving stomp to the midsection, the guard advanced on the big guy, pushing him to the corner of the room. The guard was reaching inside his suit coat for his own gun when the second man came into the room and grabbed him from behind in a bear hug. In the ensuing tussle, the two men collided with the bed, sending it against the wall with a screech of protest from its fixed casters.

A cowering Olman gasped as his plastered arm banged against the wall. The pain appeared to spur him to action, for he grabbed the call button and frantically thumbed it.

At the ward desk, the orderly glanced at the blinking red light on the control panel and back to the pretty nurse. 'You going to get that?' As he spoke, he ran a caressing hand up and down her arm.

She smiled at him and then looked at the screen and screwed up her nose. 'It's Olman, *again*. He presses that button every five minutes. I'm over it! He can wait.' Batting her lashes at the orderly, she said sweetly, 'Now what were you saying about Melissa and that new surgeon?'

Back in the room, the first islander had recovered from his beating and went on the attack again, only to receive another stomp to the midsection from the guard, who was struggling to free his arms from his second attacker's vice-like grip. He managed to reach behind to claw at his captor's groin. Grabbing a handful, he squeezed as hard as he could and heard the man give a gasp of pain. But although the big guy loosened his grip, he also brought up an arm to put the guard's neck in a headlock.

The leader had been watching proceedings with growing impatience. Stepping in from the side, he landed a solid blow on the guard's temple, followed in quick succession by another, and then another. Feeling his captive go limp, the second man clamped both large hands around the guard's head and reefed it sideways, breaking his neck with a sickening crack as the body slumped to the floor.

A sudden quiet descended on the room. The trio turned and fixed dark, insolent eyes on Olman. Hard up against the bedhead nursing his broken arm, he was still desperately thumbing the call button with his other hand. When the leader shook his head and wagged a finger at him, Olman dropped the button, raised his hand as if in surrender, and pleaded, 'I'm an important p-person. I'll pay you anything, whatever you w-want. I have money … *please!'*

The leader's only response was to bark, 'Watch the door,' to his two burly companions, who promptly moved out into the corridor.

'That's right, people are coming,' Olman cried, waving a trembling hand toward the sound of raised voices some distance away down the corridor. 'You'd better g-go.'

Throwing him a mocking grin, the leader drawled, 'This won't take long,' and took the knife from the sheath still tucked into the back of his waist band.

The overhead light glinted off the blade as he advanced toward the bed.

# CHAPTER ELEVEN

At the front door of Davidson's mansion Modeen signalled to Wolf, who loped across the carpark and pressed himself against the wall beside her. She whispered, 'Locked. See if we can find a key.'

He ran his hands across the head of the door jamb while she checked under the doormat.

Nothing.

At Wolf's murmured, 'Meter box around the corner,' she nodded and slipped around to open the box. Seeing a faded Ergon Energy pamphlet lying there, she lifted it and breathed, 'Bingo.'

Throwing the key to Wolf, she followed him to the front door and then put a hand on his burly arm. 'Wait a second.' Pulling the black pouch from her back pocket, she unfolded it and took out a small pair of wire cutters. 'Security Alarm. We should have about ten to fifteen seconds to disable it.'

Wolf nodded and slipped the key into the lock. Holding the Glock in his other hand he looked at her. 'Ready?' At her nod he turned the key and bounded through the open door.

Following close behind him, Modeen hurried to the security panel on the wall to her right. It flashed *Enter Code*. Moving swiftly, she opened the nearest internal door, which turned out to be a hallway cupboard. Flicking on the light, she spotted the security control box mounted on the back wall of the cupboard.

Recalling her NatSec training, she put both hands on the lip of the box's flimsy plastic cover and pried it open. Removing the back-up battery connector from the main circuit board, she cut the sixteen volt transformer feed. Hurrying back around to the control panel, she was relieved to see the display fade and die.

In the entrance foyer, Wolf was staring at the motion detector. As its red LED faded and went out, he glanced at Modeen with a proud grin and murmured into his comms, 'Nice work.'

Spooky moved along the outer wall to the next window. Behind it the small storeroom was packed with cartons of beer, wine and spirits. He looked hopefully up at the ceiling but then clicked his tongue. Another active motion detector blinked at him.

With a frustrated frown he was about to turn away when out of the corner of his eye he noticed the LED fade and go out. When it stayed out, he moved swiftly to the side door again and looked inside. The detector in the laundry was dead too.

Smashing the door's glass quarter panel with his elbow, he reached in, unlocked the door and slipped inside. Commencing a sweep of the bottom level, he found an expansive central room decked out with a full bar and surround sound music station, and flanked by two guest rooms on either side.

The views through the central room's floor-to-ceiling windows encompassed the infinity pool and the waters of the inlet beyond.

Moving on to the guest rooms, he found each one decked out with a king-sized bed, ensuite with spa bath, and super-sized flat-screen TV. Climbing the toughened glass and ornately balustraded stairs to the next level, he carried on with his inspection, moving quietly, leading with his Glock. Spying movement on the central level, he froze for a brief instant and then moved toward it.

'This doesn't feel right,' Modeen murmured when the three of them came together. 'A place of this size and extravagance … you'd expect *someone* to be around.'

Spooky nodded. 'I know what you mean.'

At the sound of approaching vehicles, they stiffened.

When Spooky turned to make his way to the

bottom level, Wolf said in a low growl, 'You got spare ammo?'

Glancing at him, Spooky patted his back pocket. 'Got a spare clip of Roosters right here.'

'You and your freakin' roosters.' Wolf raised an eyebrow and shook his head in reluctant amusement.

Grinning, Modeen turned to Wolf. 'I guess you and I should greet our visitors.'

With a graceful sweep of a brawny arm and a bow of his head, he drawled, 'Lead the way, Mrs Ryan.'


As Sergeant Bellamy and three of his officers burst in through the front door, they found Wolf and Modeen standing calmly eyeing them from the front foyer, pistols trained on their visitors. On recognising the sergeant, they holstered their weapons. Bellamy glared belligerently at them and barked, 'You got a warrant to search these premises?'

Raising an eyebrow, Wolf growled, 'You know better than to go there, Bellamy. We don't need a warrant, a fact you're well aware of.'

Seeing Wolf move toward him, Bellamy pulled a Glock from his side holster. He aimed it at Wolf and Modeen as the other officers stepped forward and followed suit.

'No warrant?' Bellamy said with a smug leer. 'Right, then. I'm arresting you for trespassing.' His leer melted, replaced by a wide-eyed look of fear as he felt something metal press against his temple.

'Here's our warrant,' Spooky said pleasantly. 'Now how about you and your friends put your weapons down.'

When Modeen and Wolf made to move, the officers beside Bellamy stood fast and kept their weapons trained on the two agents. One of them bellowed, 'Don't move!'

Putting his mouth closer to Bellamy's ear, Spooky hissed, 'You and your men drop your weapons *now.*'

When the three officers looked to their sergeant for direction, Wolf and Modeen took advantage of the distraction. Stepping forward they slapped their hands around the two closest officers' pistols and disarmed them in one fluid motion.

While pushing them out of the way, Wolf trained his gun on Bellamy, as Modeen stepped in and pressed Walt against the remaining officer's temple.

Spooky pushed the muzzle of his gun more firmly against Bellamy's pudgy face, making a white ring in the flushed skin. 'What's it gonna be, Bellamy?' Seeing the sergeant's pistol arm begin to shake, Spooky started counting down, 'One … two … and…,' He watched Bellamy's arm go limp and fall to his side. Taking the gun from his loose grip, Spooky said cheerily, 'Good decision.'

Modeen had already relieved the remaining officer of his weapon. Stepping back, she raised her voice. 'All of you, take off your utility belts and drop them and your phones to the floor.'

As they complied, Wolf kicked their phones to the corner of the room and collected their belts, removing the handcuffs as he did so.

'You're in big trouble,' Bellamy muttered through tense, down-turned lips as Spooky relaxed the pressure on his temple.

'Somehow I don't think so. Tell me, how did you know we were here?' Lowering his gun, Spooky prodded Bellamy in the ribs with it. 'You're in this up to your elbows, aren't you Bellamy?'

'What are you suggesting?' Bellamy blustered. 'You … you tripped the alarm, that's how we knew.'

'Oh … I don't think so.' Spooky's mouth was smiling but his eyes were sharp.

Wolf cuffed Bellamy's hands behind his back and frisked him. Pushing him toward the nearest police officer, Wolf barked, 'Turn round.' After threading one of the officer's arms through Bellamy's, he cuffed them back to back. He did the same with the remaining officers until they were all cuffed and daisy-chained back-to-back in a circle. 'Now sit down.'

There was a moment of outraged huffing and indecisive scuffling as they tried to co-ordinate their movements. Despite their attempts to maintain some vestige of dignity, they ended up crashing to the floor in a loud, cursing heap.

Spooky stood watch over them as Modeen and

Wolf continued their search of the house. Fifteen minutes later they returned to the main foyer.

'Let's make tracks.' Wolf indicated the door with a tilt of his dark head. 'We'll leave these guys here for the Feds to pick up.'

Hearing that, Bellamy let loose a string of expletives and roared, 'You can't just leave us here, handcuffed like this!'

Spooky threw him a withering glance and continued gathering up their belts and phones. 'We're not like you, Bellamy. We'll get someone to pick you up later. Oh, and if I were you, I'd get myself a good lawyer.'

As they made for the door, he passed their phones to Modeen saying in a low voice, 'Check out the phone on top. That's Bellamy's, and it looks like he received a text from Davidson with the entry code for the gate.'

'Did he now?' She crinkled her chin thoughtfully. 'Well, that might give us enough reason to hold them both in custody for a while. But we'll need more evidence before they can be charged with anything.'


As they strode past the two police cars parked diagonally in the driveway, Wolf and Modeen reached into the drivers' sides and removed the keys from the ignitions. When her phone buzzed, Modeen pulled it from the side pocket of her cargo pants and looked at the caller ID. 'It's Ben.' Pressing Answer, she placed the phone to her ear.

'Where are you?' Ben rapped, his tone one of urgency.

'At the East Trinity property as instructed. What's up?'

'I've just got off the plane in Cairns. Foster has been broken out of Federal Police custody. And that's not all.' He paused briefly. 'The premier has been assassinated in his bed at the hospital and six federal officers have been killed, two at the hospital and four at the Federal Headquarters.'

Modeen stopped in her tracks. Closing her eyes, she exhaled and hung her head. Seeing that, Wolf and Spooky also halted.

Ben's voice steadied. 'Both places were hit at the same time by men described as large and of Islander descent, who were then seen driving away in black Ford sedans.'

Lifting her head, Modeen said quietly, 'Do you want us back in Cairns?'

'No. I think they accomplished what they came here to do. My guess is they're either heading to Julia Creek or are on their way to East Trinity.'

'Thanks for the heads-up. I'll call you back ASAP.' Putting her phone away she turned to the others. 'We need to take cover. There could be more company heading this way.' Keeping low she led them back behind the police cars. 'Olman was assassinated at the hospital and Foster's been broken out. Six federal officers were killed in the process.'

Wolf and Spooky shook their heads and frowned.

'Ben thinks the perpetrators may be on their way here,' Modeen continued. 'They're driving black Ford sedans.'

Spooky threw her a significant glance. 'Black Mambas?'

'More than likely.'

'Should we wait for them here or head to Townsville?'

Modeen fixed Wolf with a level gaze. 'It's a four hour drive, and we don't have to be there 'til one in the morning.' She gnawed her bottom lip, her even teeth white against the pink plumpness. 'I guess we can afford to hang around here for a bit and see if they show. In the meantime, I reckon we should move our car away from the front gate. Don't want to give them any sort of heads-up.'

'I could grab the sniper rifle out'the boot and cover their approach from the roof.' Wolf raised his eyebrows at her and she nodded.

Spooky dropped the officers' utility belts on the ground and held out a hand. 'You got the keys, Modeen? I know the security code for the gate.'

She dug into her pocket and handed him the keys to the BMW. Skirting around the patrol car, he disappeared into the thick foliage on the right of the driveway.

Seeing Modeen frown and stare down the path, Wolf asked, 'What's wrong?'

'We're too late.' She tugged her Walther PPQ from its holster as she spoke. 'I just got a whiff of reefer smoke.'

Giving a whistle to warn Spooky, Wolf pulled out his Glock. Taking one of the officers' weapons from the pile of utility belts, he checked the clip, locked and loaded the pistol and then handed it to Modeen. 'I'll flank 'em on the left of the driveway.' Grabbing another Glock from the pile of utility belts, he ducked off as, a second later, a black Ford sedan appeared around the corner.

The driver could be seen wincing as the low-riding suspension of the heavily loaded vehicle scraped over raised parts of the winding driveway.

Breaking cover, Modeen walked casually toward the car, a welcoming smile on her face and both hands behind her back. Seeing her, the driver accelerated and then brought the vehicle to a stop ten metres in front of her.

Nobody moved for a long moment.

Taking a drag on their joints, the two heavy-set men in the back seat leaned their tattoo-covered faces forward to peer between the front bucket seats. The equally tattooed driver and front passenger slowly returned Modeen's smile, their white teeth shining through thick, dark lips. But when the driver reached for the pistol lying in plain view on the dashboard, his smile became a grimace. He ducked, shielding his face with a meaty arm, as Modeen put four bullets through the windscreen while sprinting toward the vehicle. Springing onto the bonnet and then the roof, she released another four rounds into the vehicle's back compartment as she went.

Sliding down the rear window, she leapt off the boot and let loose two more rounds through the window as she skidded to a stop five metres behind the vehicle.

During her assault Wolf and Spooky had broken cover. They jogged toward the sedan, guns raised. The stocky man seated behind the driver opened the back door, bracing himself while attempting to exit the vehicle holding a sawn-off double barrel shotgun.

Dropping to one knee, Wolf peppered him with nine millimetre bullets, nailing him back in his seat.

On the other side of the car Spooky approached with caution and checked the occupants. Three were obviously dead, twisted and bloody in their seats, two still strapped in by their seatbelts. The front passenger coughed and gurgled, clutching his throat with both hands and fighting for breath. Blood gushed between his fingers and dribbled from the corners of his mouth, mixed with frothy saliva. He convulsed in his seat, straining to look sideways at Spooky. Then his eyes went dull and his head slumped forward on his flaccid neck.

Modeen kept her weapon trained on the driveway

in case of more arrivals while Spooky and Wolf finished checking the vehicle.

'Foster wasn't with them,' Wolf announced as they walked up to her. 'The boot's full of assorted ammo, rifles, RPGs and grenades. There's even a Maximi.' He shook his head. 'Pretty sophisticated weaponry to be carrying in the boot of a passenger vehicle.'

Modeen lowered Walt and faced him. 'I reckon that'd be Reger and Foster's influence.' She turned to Spooky. 'Grab the car, Spook and I'll call it in.'

Holding up a box of nine millimetre cartridges, Spooky grinned and threw the box to Wolf. 'These roosters might come in handy.' Still grinning, he headed down the driveway.

Catching the box in his right hand, Wolf bent and tucked it into the small canvas bag he'd collected from the boot of the sedan, mumbling, *'Again* with the freakin' roosters....'

# CHAPTER TWELVE

In the premier's room at the Cairns Private Hospital, Ben moved quietly around the group of forensic officers hovering at Olman's bedside. Stepping over the premier's personal bodyguard, now sprawled motionless on the floor, Ben glanced at the body lying across the bloodstained sheets.

Olman's head was wedged back and against the bedhead by the hilt of a ten inch knife which protruded from his bottom jaw. His wide, startled eyes stared unseeingly upward. Moving closer, Ben peered at the weapon. The dark image of a black mamba snake had been scorched into the wooden handle. Straightening, he turned and strode out into the ward. When his mobile rang he put it to his ear and barked, 'Go ahead, JD.'

Modeen launched straight into her report. 'We had visitors as you suspected. Four men in a black late model Ford arrived at Davidson's East Trinity residence and confronted us. They have been neutralised,' she said flatly. 'Foster was not among them. We believe they were tipped off about our presence there by one Sergeant Bellamy, who arrived at the location just before they did with three other officers, all of whom we've restrained at the residence.'

'Good work, JD, I'll inform the Feds and get them to arrange Davidson's apprehension. As this is their turf and they've lost six of their own, I'm sure they'll be only too eager to collar Bellamy and the others. I'll try to assist them as much as I can here.' Ben paused and lowered his voice. 'As far as Julia Creek goes, I think it's best if we keep that to ourselves for the time being. And don't forget there were *two* black sedans. We've only accounted for one so far.'

'Copy that.'

With a crunch of tyres on gravel, Spooky pulled up beside Modeen in the M3 sedan. The wheels had only just stopped turning as Wolf climbed into the back, allowing Modeen, phone still to her ear, to slip into the front next to Spooky.

'The three of us are Oscar Mike, heading to Townsville.'

'Good.' There was a nod in Ben's voice. 'Keep me apprised of your progress.'

'Will do.'

'By the way, I ran into Kevin Simpson, who wanted

me to let you know he's been discharged from hospital and is heading back to Brisbane.'

'Good to hear, thanks.' Modeen pressed End Call and nodded to Spooky and then to Wolf. 'There were two black Ford sedans, so we'd better keep a vigil for the other one.'

On the Bruce Highway heading south, Spooky set the cruise control at the speed limit, one hundred kilometres an hour, and stretched. 'Settle in guys, we got a long trip ahead of us.'

As they passed through Cardwell a while later, he commented on how well the tiny coastal township had recovered after the devastation of cyclone Yasi. Climbing the Cardwell range, he said, 'Check out the views to Hinchinbrook Island,' only to realise the other two were asleep. 'Oh great, I'm talking to myself.'

Pulling into MacDonald's in Ingham a short time later, Spooky nosed the BMW into the nearest parking bay, saying loudly, 'Who wants a coffee?'

The other two stirred, yawning and stretching and then all three got out. At Wolf's, 'What'll you have?' Modeen ordered a double-shot flat white and a burger. When the two men headed inside to place their order, she found a quiet table outside where they could sit with their backs to the wall and have a clear view of the patrons' comings and goings. Five minutes later

Wolf passed Modeen her order as he and Spooky joined her at the table.

'A double shot Modeen, I'm impressed.'

'You know what they say, Spook,' she replied.

'No, what?'

'Go hard or go home.'

He gave a bark of laughter. 'But we're gonna have to wean ourselves off Maccas one day.'

Modeen raised a lazy eyebrow at him and purred, 'Why?'

'Yeah, frig that, Spook,' Wolf growled.

'Just sayin'….' Spooky took a sip of coffee. 'I ran into Dozer a while ago. You guys remember how fit he was back in the unit?

Modeen nodded. 'And?'

'Well I met him about a month ago in a Maccas North of Perth, and I gotta say, he was so fat and outta shape, I reckon he'd have trouble wiping his own—'

Modeen thrust a hand in the air and gave a vigorous shake of her head. 'Enough!' She pulled a face. 'I think we get the picture. And don't you be bagging Maccas, they've served us well over the years. Besides….'

Making a fist, she then extended her index finger. 'A: Maccas is one of the few places that's open twenty-four by seven which is very handy in our line of work.' She extended her middle finger. 'And B: when you exercise and stay as active as we do, you burn off whatever you eat.'

Spooky was about to speak when Modeen extended a third finger. 'And C....' She paused to watch a patron emerge from the fast food restaurant carrying a tray of thick shakes and french fries. 'The coffee and burgers aren't bad.' She lowered her hand and sat back. 'And thus ends the lesson.'

A grinning Spooky gave a submissive shrug of his compact, muscular shoulders.

'Yeah, so shut-up and eat,' Wolf growled. 'I don't remember having any lunch, and right now I'm starving.'


Back in the car, Modeen took the driver's seat for the remaining eighty minute journey to Townsville. Beside her Spooky rested his head against the door and closed his eyes, while in the rear-view mirror she saw Wolf's head nodding as the car carried them smoothly toward their destination.

When the day stretched into dusk, she turned on the headlights and the beams glanced off the pale grey water pipe snaking through the dry, scrubby growth and hugging the entire length of the road. At a soft snore from the back seat, she found her thoughts straying to the future.

But that was dangerous territory, so she switched her mind back to the mission.

A while later Spooky lifted his head and stretched. Blinking at the approaching lights of Townsville, he yawned and rubbed his face. 'Well, that was a pretty uneventful trip.' He glanced at Modeen. 'I guess the second black sedan took an alternate route, hey?'

'I certainly didn't see them.' Modeen kept her eyes on the road. 'They could've gone past while we were at Davidson's place. Or they might've gone west through Conjuboy on the Kennedy Development Road ... not that it matters really. I have a feeling we'll be meeting up with them at Julia Creek.'

The traffic thickened as they neared the city. Leaving the arterial road that skirted the CBD, they turned into Ingham Road. This took them alongside the RAAF base, where they glimpsed a C17 Globemaster on the tarmac.

Even at a distance the enormous plane dominated the area, dwarfing all the other aircraft parked nearby.

An old Iroquois helicopter, mothballed and looking somehow pathetic and dejected now it was no longer in service, sat on a remote patch of lawn close to the high steel-mesh security fence that encircled the base.

'Turn left here,' Spooky instructed. 'The main entrance is just after that Mosquito.'

'Mosquito?' Modeen peered at the silver-grey aircraft mounted on permanent display at the front of the complex and raised an eyebrow. 'That's a Lockheed P-2 Neptune.'

Spooky's face went blank and then he blushed. 'Oh ... right, a Neptune. Yeah, well that would've been my second guess.'

Wolf reached forward to thump him on the arm. 'Don't feel bad, mate, they do look similar … sort of.'

Turning into the main entrance, they followed the road around and stopped in front of a boom gate attached to a small brick guard house, where a watching guard stood waiting for them. He studied their NatSec badges carefully and then waved them through the solid white security gates, directing them to report to the main administration building on the right.

They pulled into a carpark in front of the nondescript three storey building. It was boringly rectangular, the only distinguishing feature its obviously seventies-style sand-coloured clay bricks.

Making their way to the front door, they paused as the roar of a fighter jet's engines reached their ears. Peering toward the runway they saw an F/A18 Super Hornet approaching from the east. Coming in low as if to land, the streamlined fighter suddenly retracted its wheels. A bright burst of flame extended from its tail followed by another ear-assaulting roar, and then it was gone.

Wolf nodded. 'Training exercises.'

'Yep.' Gazing into the sky after the disappearing speck, Spooky grinned. 'We're in the right place.'

As they filed into the building and fronted up to the reception counter, a middle-aged woman in a blue Air Force uniform, hair pulled back in a tight bun, looked up from a nearby desk and rose to greet them.

After eyeing each of them in turn, she smiled as though in recognition and said pleasantly, 'Are you here for the 5$^{th}$ Aviation Regiment?' Seeing Modeen's nod, the woman picked up the phone and pressed three numbers for an internal extension. After a moment she announced, 'Your visitors have arrived,' and then listened for a second before putting down the phone. 'Gary will be with you shortly.' She indicated chairs gathered around a coffee table in a corner of the waiting room. 'Please make yourselves comfortable.'

They moved over to the chairs but didn't sit, preferring to stand after the hours spent in the car. Spooky picked up one of the brightly-coloured, appealing recruitment pamphlets from off the coffee table and flicked through its glossy pages.

Minutes later a young lieutenant in a khaki uniform strolled over to them and extended a hand to Wolf, who was nearest. 'Gary Hawkins, A Squadron.' He shook hands with the other two and then motioned them all toward the door. 'We'll get you kitted out and squared away. Please follow me.'

At Wolf's drawled, 'Great service,' Hawkins grinned.

'We've been expecting you, Mr Ryan.' He led them out of the building and onto the runway apron, where they piled into an Army G-Wagon. As he drove toward a well maintained but clearly wartime-constructed weatherboard dormitory behind the admin building, he announced, 'You'll be able to shower and change here. Unfortunately the mess is closed, but your colleague managed to put some rations aside for you.'

All three frowned and Spooky piped up, 'What colleague?'

'He's been waiting to brief you in the common room. I'll take you straight there and he can give you an orientation.'

Hearing that, they shared an inquisitive glance and then shrugged as Hawkins pulled the G-wagon into a bay outside the low-stumped Queenslander-styled building.

Leading them to the dormitory, he held open the first door to the right of the foyer. 'I'll be back at twenty-four hundred hours to collect you all.' Waiting just long enough for them to go through, he turned and strode away.

As they entered the common room, a familiar rangy figure with a strawberry blonde flat-top rose from where he'd been leaning against one of the tables and flashed them a toothy grin.

Striding over to him, they fist-bumped and all four chanted, 'Who dares wins!' before laughing and thumping each other on the back.

'We should've known it'd be you.' Modeen grinned into his tightly-crinkled murky blue eyes. 'Great to see you again, Bugs. Though it feels like only yesterday we were all in Kabul.'

Bugs beamed back at her. 'Might feel like only

yesterday, Modeen, but it was over twelve months ago, can you believe it.'

She shook her head in disbelief as Wolf drawled, 'I'm surprised you don't have that big fella with you, Karim was it? I thought Ben was keen to sign him up when he finished his tour. He was mighty handy at close quarters combat.'

Bugs' expression sobered and his tone grew sombre. 'He would've been, but….' He sighed and ran a hand over his buzz-cut hair. 'Karim was on a recon mission with a small team of commandos, when the Black Hawk they were in was shot down by a ground-to-air missile. Karim survived the crash and managed to pull the crew from the wreckage, only to be cut down by ground fire.' He paused as the other three shook their heads sadly.

Spooky put a hand on his shoulder. 'Sorry to hear that mate, he was a good soldier.'

Bugs gazed around at his three friends. 'We've lost a lot of mates and good soldiers over the years. I guess it's just the nature of the beast.' The others nodded as he went on. 'And the conflict in the Middle East has escalated. Terrorist forces have been boosted by the influx of crack foreign fighters. These new recruits are well armed, well trained, and vicious. They also have a strong network behind them. They've taken Ramadi, and the Iraqi troops battling them are on the back foot.'

They shared a sombre moment and then Bugs' face brightened. 'I'll show you to your quarters. You can freshen up and change into your night ops gear. I left containers of food from the mess on top of the bunks in your rooms in case you're hungry.' He glanced at his watch. 'We'll meet back here at twenty-two hundred and go over the mission.'

Wolf knocked on the door and heard, 'It's open,' from within. Entering the room he saw Modeen on her bunk, hair still damp from her shower and the smell of soap and shampoo lingering on the air. Dressed in black cargo pants, combat boots and black T-shirt, she was lying back, arms crossed behind her head.

'You're early.'

'Yeah. I was ready, so….' Dumping his black duffel packed with night ops gear in the corner next to her bag, he said, 'Whatcha doin'?' The thread of tension in his voice had her sitting up to look more closely at him. 'Just marking time before the mission.' She watched as he pulled out the chair from the small desk, spun it around and set it down in front of the bunk. Taking a seat facing her, he rested his arms on top of the backrest. She found herself holding her breath, as though sensing something was coming.

'The last few days have been pretty hectic....' His eyes locked on hers and then he looked away, running a hand over his tousled hair. His gravelly voice was deeper than usual, and it felt like he was choosing his words carefully when he continued. 'So I thought … this might be a good time to have a chat. Before we go to the briefing.'

Feeling a pre-emptive flutter of nerves in her stomach, she smiled, trying to keep things light. 'Sounds serious.' Shuffling back on the bunk, she leaned against the wall.

'Yes … well … I am serious.' Pausing to take a deep breath, he locked eyes with her and went on in a rush. 'I want you to marry me, Jo.'

She froze and then her jaw dropped. She stayed like that for what seemed to him like a full minute and then she sat bolt upright. 'You *what?*'

This time when he said the words he sounded calmer, more in control, as though the worst was over. 'I want you to marry me.'

'You're serious?'

'Deadly serious.'

She continued gaping at him. 'You choose *now* to ask me that?'

'Yeah, not the best timing I know. But in our line of work, if I waited for the perfect moment—'

'In our line of work.' Forcing herself to move, she

threw her hands in the air. '*Exactly* why this would be a bad idea.'

He shook his head and his firm lips tipped into a shy smile, one that softened his face in a way she'd never seen before. 'No, it's a *good* idea … if we make this our last mission.'

Staring at him, she said slowly, 'Our last mission? You mean … give up our jobs? Leave NatSec?'

'Yep, drop off the radar after this and start a normal life. I could get a mining job out the back of Woop-woop, truck driving or labouring, or *anything* really. It won't worry me what I do … as long as we're together, you and me.'

The intensity in his voice and in his gaze took her breath away. Searching for something to say to defuse the situation, she murmured, 'This is all a bit sudden....'

'It might seem like that to you, but I've been thinking about it for a while now.' There was that shy smile again. Her heart turned over as he went on. 'We've both had some close calls, and I … don't want to lose you.'

She frowned. 'Did my being shot at in Cairns bring this on?'

'No, like I said, I've been thinking about this – *wanting* this – for a while. What happened in Cairns was just a spur for me to act.' Rising to his feet, he pushed the chair aside and moved to stand in front of her bunk, gazing down at her tenderly. 'Being a sniper, I know better than anyone that in our line of work a bullet can come out of nowhere, at anytime. I could've lost you….'

His voice broke and he blinked hard. Looking down at the floor, he took a moment to regain his composure. Lifting his chin, he said firmly, 'I guess what I'm saying is, if you feel the same way about me as I do about you, then let's call it quits and get out while we can.'

When she didn't respond, simply stared wide-eyed at him, he sighed. 'Just do me a favour and think about it.' Holding out his arms, he helped her up from the bed.

Standing in front of him, his strong hands on her arms and their bodies almost touching, she gazed up at him. 'You know I….' She swallowed. 'You know how I feel about you, Troy.'

When he lifted the gold chain from around his neck and placed it over her head, she glanced down and saw a rose gold ring dangling from the base of the chain.

Grasping it, she brought the ring closer to her face. The overhead light sparkled off the diamonds embedded around the band. Meeting his eyes again, she gave a slow smile. With a satisfied nod, Wolf slid his hands gently down her arms and stepped away.

Bending to collect his duffel, he said in a more normal voice, 'Time for the mission brief.'

Slipping the chain inside her shirt, she grabbed her duffel and followed him out the door.

They didn't speak on their way to the common room, where they found Bugs and Spooky sitting at a central table, mugs of coffee in front of them.

Seeing them enter, Bugs tilted his head toward the kitchenette. 'The kettle's just boiled.'

Dropping his duffel in a corner, Wolf strode over to take two cups from the shelf above the sink. Glancing at Modeen, who nodded, he drawled, 'I'll take that as a white with one,' and they shared a small smile.

As she took a seat at the table her expression grew serious. 'Is this a secure location to be discussing mission parameters?'

Bugs glanced at her. 'Relax. We're the only ones in this wing.' He grinned. 'I was just tellin' Spook here that I've put in for a transfer back to Oz. Ben gave it the OK and said he'll start looking for a replacement straight away.'

'What happens if he can't find one?' Wolf asked over the rumble of the kettle coming back to the boil.

Bugs glanced over at him. 'I told him I could hold out for another three months if necessary.'

'Where will you be stationed here?'

'Melbourne temporarily, 'til a more permanent opening comes up elsewhere. And that suits me, it's an easy trip to Adelaide from there.'

'I thought you liked it in Kabul?' Picking up the two steaming mugs, Wolf brought them to the table and set one in front of Modeen before taking a seat opposite her.

Bugs nodded. 'It was OK for a while, but right now family calls.'

'Family?' Stealing a glance at Modeen, Wolf found her looking thoughtfully back at him. He turned to Bugs. 'What's the go?'

'Well, my folks aren't gettin' any younger, and the ex is having trouble keepin' our young bloke in line.' He gave a toothy grin. 'Seems Cam takes after his no-good father.'

This met with amused snorts from around the table as Bugs went on. 'I reckon the timing's right too to get out of there. There's more foreign troops floodin' into Kabul all the time as anti-terrorist campaigns ramp up. The US military base in Bagram's burstin' at the seams with US, French 'n Aussie fighter bombers, and now even the Ruskies are wadin' into the fight.

'It's gettin' too crowded, and my presence there isn't as important as it once was. Anyway, there's enough goin' on here to keep us all occupied.' He unfolded a map and laid it on the table, smoothing out the creases with his freckled hands. 'Right, down to business.'

The others gathered around.

'As you know, the target is an alleged meths lab at Julia Creek,' and he pointed to a remote spot on the map. 'We'll parachute in tonight, using the HAHO special ops chutes Ben's organised. He's arranged for a Taipan to drop us forty kilometres from the station. We'll deploy at twenty-five thousand feet and glide in under cover of darkness. The Hi-Glide chutes have a glide ratio of six to one, so all going well, they should put us on the ground within five clicks of the property. We'll cover the rest of the distance on foot.' Reaching for his laptop, he opened it and brought up a satellite image of the cattle station.

Peering at the screen, Spooky muttered, 'Looks harmless enough.'

Bugs gave a snort. 'Look again.' When he zoomed in on a large barn at the back of the homestead, what appeared at first to be two balconies at each end of the structure revealed themselves to be makeshift gun turrets. Clicking on the screen, he brought up a heat signature overlay.

'At the time this image was captured, they must've been cookin' a batch of meths, as the dominant heat source is smack-bang in the centre of the barn. And see here?' and he pointed at the turrets. 'Looks to me like they're armed with Maximis.'

The other three exchanged glances and Modeen nodded at Bugs.

'That's highly likely. The aggressors we ran into in Cairns had a Maximi in the boot of their black Ford sedan.'

'So they're packin' some serious weaponry.' Bugs

brought up another heat image. 'This was taken three hours ago and shows roughly twenty-eight people on the station.'

'There!' Wolf pointed to a spot on the screen. 'Zoom in to the left side of the homestead.'

Bugs ran his finger over the laptop's built-in mouse pad and zoomed in on two dark dots. They proved to be black sedans, their front bonnets emitting a dull red hue from the warm engines beneath.

Modeen peered at them closely. 'They can't be the two that were in Cairns. For a start, we immobilised one, and if the other left the area around the same time, it'd still be in transit.' She sat back looking pensive, and then said gravely, 'So I reckon you can count on there being thirty-two or even more at the Julia Creek property.'

Bugs stared at her for a moment, deep in thought, and then said, 'We've been up against worse odds. And intel suggests a number of them will be lab technicians and non-hostiles. That's why Ben wants us to infiltrate the property, identify and remove the hostiles, and destroy the lab. On the plus side, we've got a fifty cal AMR, three F90s, the latest military comms units built into our combat helmets, and six C4 charges.'

'Are the F90s fitted with suppressors?'

'Nah Spook, unfortunately they're not. So for stealth and close quarters, you'll have to use your sidearm … or get creative.' Bugs threw him a wink.

'We've got a Lapua Magnum in the boot of our

vehicle,' Wolf drawled. 'Considering the flat terrain and low vegetation, I suggest we have two snipers to cover the compound.' He tapped a finger on two points of the map. 'One here, covering the southeast, the other the southwest. From these positions we should be able to cover both turrets and the homestead, and spot anyone making a run for it.'

'Good.' Modeen rose to her feet. 'Spooky and I'll set the charges while you and Bugs cover our six.'

Wolf frowned at her. 'Hang on, I—'

'We need you on the fifty cal,' she said crisply, 'and Bugs on the Lapua.'

'That's fine by me.' Patting a scowling Wolf on the back, Bugs got to his feet and began folding the map, as a knock came on the door and Hawkins entered the room.

'The chopper's being prepped for lift-off in forty minutes. If you'll come with me I'll take you to collect your chutes on the way to the helipad.'

When Modeen said, 'We'll need to collect some gear from our vehicle on the way,' he barked, 'Sure no problem,' and hastened to open the door for them.

Catching the obvious 'hurry up' drift, Bugs snapped his laptop closed. 'Right, well that's the basic plan. As we all know, things don't always go to plan, so be ready to improvise. Any questions or issues?'

When no one else spoke, Spooky announced, 'Looks like we're good to go.'

# CHAPTER FOURTEEN

At o-one hundred, an MRH90 Taipan sat on the helipad behind the aircraft hangars on the northern side of Townsville airbase, while its two pilots, armed with torches, completed their final pre-flight checks in the dark.

Replacing the Australian Defence Force's aging Blackhawks and Sea Kings, the sixteen metre-long, multi-role Taipan, weighing over six ton and accommodating up to eighteen fully kitted soldiers, boasted the latest in technology including fly-by-wire systems.

As Hawkins pulled the G-Wagon to the perimeter of the helipad, his passengers tried to catch a glimpse of the aircraft that was about to transport them into the state's remote western region. Its camouflage combat colours were lost in the darkness, but a faint light illuminated the helicopter's interior cargo hold.

The four disembarked and double-timed across the

tarmac to the waiting Taipan. Throwing their chutes and kit into the chopper's huge cargo hold, they climbed aboard. While the others made themselves comfortable, Bugs went forward to the cockpit and confirmed coordinates and radio comms with the pilots.

'About two hours flying time,' he said on his return, a wide, toothy grin his only distinguishing feature in the low light. He leaned against the corner of the cargo hold. 'Pilots will be doing manoeuvres out of Mount Isa and will be on stand-by if they're needed.'

His last words were lost in the whir of the awakening twin Rolls-Royce Turbomeca engines. The four huge rotor blades above the cabin began chopping through the air as the four in the cargo hold synchronised watches and settled in for the trip.

Moments later the Taipan lifted off the ground, nose down, and hovered briefly before turning west and powering away at speed.

Zooming low over the landscape, they cleared the outer hills of the city as the chopper accelerated to two hundred and eighty kilometres an hour. The drone of its engine settled into a dull roar as Modeen leaned across to Bugs.

'Did it ever occur to you,' she yelled above the noise, 'that Reger and Foster might be alive, given what we now know about Gator?'

When he leaned forward to reply, a dull red light from the cockpit gave his buzz-cut hair an extra crimson hue. 'Nah. I never met 'em. Guess I was only focused on Gator 'cos he was part of our old unit.'

Modeen nodded. 'Same with us, but we were hoping you might know who and what we'll be up against.'

Shrugging and raising his hands palms-up in a *no idea* gesture, Bugs paused and dropped his hands again. Leaning forward once more, he raised his voice.

'All I know is what Ben told me, that these guys are hard-core military who won't think twice about cutting our throats.' Reaching out, he touched Modeen's hand for emphasis. 'So we can't afford to give 'em an inch.'

Hearing that, Wolf grasped her arm and gently pulled her closer beside him. Putting his mouth against her ear, he murmured, 'Let me set the charges.'

Modeen pulled back to fix her eyes squarely on his. 'You're our best sniper, why would you want to do that? And why change our agreed strategy all of a sudden?'

'I've got a bad feeling about this mission.'

She stared at him for a long moment and then leaned in close, her breath warm against his ear. 'This is going to take all four of us, and we'll need your skills as a sniper to succeed. Those skills have saved us on more than one occasion.' Pulling back, she fixed her eyes on his again. 'Besides, the bloke I plan to marry respects my abilities as a solider. I could never marry a needy wuss.' She shook her head but her eyes were smiling.

At her words his face brightened. Glancing across at Bugs and Spooky, he growled, 'Right, let's suit up.'

The cargo hold became a hive of activity as the four donned their chutes, strapping their rifles and night ops gear onto their webbing. They were completing final checks of each other's kit when the warning alarm sounded and a red display on the bulkhead flashed *Deploy*. Bugs went to check with the pilots while the others stood in the cargo bay's opening and gazed into the blackness of the night sky.

On his return, Bugs barked, 'Put your masks on. We're climbing to twenty-five thousand feet and as soon as we reach that altitude, we jump.' Pulling his miniature breathing apparatus over his nose and mouth, he held out the small GPS that was secured to his wrist via a lanyard. The others looked at the white arrow in the centre of the screen. It pointed to their destination while the readout below indicated the distance to target.

*Thirty-eight kilometres.*

They felt the powerful surge of the motors as the Taipan continued to climb.

Moments later it levelled out and the red *Deploy* display turned to solid green. Before the warning buzzer could commence its more urgent pulse, Bugs stepped up to the cargo bay's opening and leapt out into the darkness, followed a heartbeat later by Wolf, Modeen and then Spooky.

Six seconds after she pulled the drogue, the main canopy of Modeen's chute unfolded, extending the eleven metre-wide elliptical ram-air wing and inflating all seventeen ribbed cells in the lining. Specifically designed for high altitude high open jumps, and mainly used for missions requiring increased stand-off, the chutes were selected by special forces for their exceptional flight performance and docile handling.

Clicking their night vision goggles onto the central mounts of their tiered combat helmets, Wolf, Spooky and Modeen followed Bugs, who used his GPS with its altimeter function to guide them to their destination and monitor their rate of descent. Even with the weight of their kit, they sailed effortlessly toward their target. With eighteen kilometres to go, their elevation was just over eleven thousand feet.

Approaching the landing zone five kilometres from the homestead, Bugs clipped his night vision goggles into place and started scanning the ground for an appropriate landing spot. Glimpsing a faint light in the distance he set his compass to it and then veered left, gliding to a landing in a patch of ground that was bare but for a speckling of low spinifex. The others dropped in behind him and reeled in their black chutes, securing them under the nearest bushes. Re-grouping, they checked their watches and comms units for the final time.

Wolf unclipped the heavy AMR fifty cal rifle from his webbing and slung it over a shoulder. Bending his helmet's mic arm closer to his mouth, he muttered, 'Wait 'til Bugs and I are in position before you approach the homestead.'

Bugs was gazing at his compass. 'I took a bearing of the station on our approach.'

Modeen nodded. 'So did we. Isn't it unusual for them to have lights burning this hour of the night? I thought most stations this far out were on generator power and had a twenty-two hundred curfew?'

They looked at each other and Bugs said in a low voice, 'They might be expecting visitors, so be careful.' He patted Wolf on the shoulder. 'You ready to go, big fella?'

With a growled, 'Ready,' Wolf turned to Modeen and Spooky. 'Give us at least ten minutes before you set off.'

Spooky replied, 'Roger,' as he and Modeen watched the two snipers weave their way into the sparsely covered bush and disappear from sight. Slinging their rifles, they checked their sidearms and Spooky held out a pair of ten inch knives, complete with calf scabbards. 'Thought you might like these, Modeen. They're well balanced and among other things, good for throwing and close quarter combat.'

She frowned at him. 'What about you?'

He tapped the side of his leg and she looked down to see he was already wearing a matching pair.

She smiled. 'How come you didn't give me these in the chopper?'

'Well … Bugs and I had a bet that Wolf might try to talk you out of coming with me.' He gave a cheesy grin.

'Yeah?' She raised an eyebrow. 'Who won the bet?'

'Let's just say Bugs owes me twenty bucks.' He laughed and gave her a fist bump. 'Easy money! He's been in Afghanistan too long, it'll do him good to be based back here in Australia. Besides, he's fun to hang out with.'

Seeing Modeen check her watch, he sobered. 'What d'ya reckon?'

'Close enough.' Her voice was clipped, business-like as she ushered him forward.

Taking the lead, he checked his compass and then strode off due west in the direction of the homestead, picking a trail through the scrub with Modeen close behind.

Wolf and Bugs made good progress, moving quickly through the semi-arid savannah country. The dry, knee-high grass gave way to stony outcrops of meso-zonic rocks and shallow red soil with Eucalypt trees dotted here and there. Peeling off at the south eastern corner, Wolf took up position on a rocky rise that afforded a strategic view of the eastern side of the homestead and beyond, to the closest turret tower. He tugged the rangefinder binoculars from his webbing and measured the distance to the tower.

*Eighteen hundred and fifty metres.*

It was o-three hundred hours and the darkness was beginning to lift. The only light he could see glowed from the front room of the homestead. Unslinging and lowering the AMR, he set up its tripod on the highest point of the outcrop.

Bugs continued westward and came to a gravel clearing delineated on either side by two windrows.

*The main road leading to the homestead. I was counting on crossing it at some stage.*

Crouching next to some thickets, he was about to break cover when a light moving in the distance caught his eye. Whispering into his comms, 'Vehicle approaching from the south,' he eased back and lay flat on his stomach.

Wolf grabbed the AMR and hunkered down on the rocky ledge. Although a good hundred metres from the road, he didn't want to chance being seen as the vehicle went past.

At the edge of the freshly graded road that encircled the property, Modeen and Spooky lay motionless in a thick patch of knee-high grass. Through their night vision goggles, the dark green hue of large fig and mango trees, no doubt planted by the original owners to provide shade for the house yard, made an impressive backdrop to the homestead.

Mumbling, 'Black Ford sedan,' Bugs bent his head

when a shower of gravel and a cloud of red dust engulfed him as the vehicle sped past.

A short distance later its brake lights came on, and Bugs heard the bump and clatter as it went over the cattle grate and into the house yard. Lifting his head he was about to get up, only to stiffen and remain stock-still where he lay. When the rustling and thumps to his right came closer, he slowly eased a hand down to grip the hilt of his bowie knife.

Sliding the blade from its sheath, he turned his head and, bunching his muscles, prepared to face the intruder. He felt sweat running down his back as the noise came closer, and then the bush in front of him shuddered and parted.

He gave a start when a small grey figure landed right in front of him. It was a Julia Creek Dunnart. Its tiny striped nose twitched as it came closer to sniff his night vision goggles. When he blinked and exhaled, the little marsupial froze and then took a giant leap backwards, and was gone.

Bugs grinned and sprang to his feet. Shoving the knife back into its sheath, he bent low and raced across the road.

# CHAPTER FIFTEEN

Through the AMR's Schmidt and Bender telescopic sight, Wolf watched the black Ford come to a stop in front of the low-set Queenslander-style homestead. The porch light flickered on as if sensing the car's presence and a tall figure emerged through the front door.

Dressed in jeans and checked shirt, the stocky man waited at the top of the stairs as all four doors of the sedan opened and four heavily-built men got out. From the centre of the back seat, a figure slid across to the driver's side and then emerged from the back door.

This man was taller and leaner, with an athleticism about his movements that his thickset companions lacked.

*Foster.*

Wolf's eyes narrowed.

*And old mate with the melon head at the top of the stairs has gotta be Reger.*

The new arrival climbed the steps nimbly and the two men shook hands. As the other four stomped up to join them, Reger acknowledged them with a nod and then all six trooped inside.

Wolf spoke into his comms. 'I just ID'd Foster and Reger. Bugs, you in position?'

The answer came straight back. 'Affirmative. I have a good field of vision to the rear yards, barn, sheds and the house. There's some activity around a semitrailer parked at the back of the ring road, and I count two guards walkin' the boundary, and one in the turret. I can just make out some sand bags at the northern end behind the main barn.'

'We can confirm that,' Spooky whispered. 'Looks like they've built a small bunker out of sand bags … but I think the guy stationed there is asleep. We've got two guards on this side, one at the back of the house, and one over near the stockyards.'

Hearing the reports, Modeen broke her silence. 'Whenever you're ready, Wolf. The sun'll be up in a couple of hours, so we'll move as soon as you take out the guard manning the eastern turret.'

Six seconds later the guard slumped sideways, cracking his head on the turret balustrade as he fell to the floor.

Up on the ridge, Wolf made two fine adjustments to the scope.

*Three inches too low and one inch to the left.*

When the other guards gave no indication of having seen or heard anything amiss, Modeen and Spooky raced across the ring road, keeping low, and crouched by the fence nearest the barn. Over the comms they heard a reassuring, 'So far, so good,' and knew Wolf was monitoring their progress from his post on the ridge.

The old barn was solidly built, its forty metre length and twenty metre width constructed of huge timber posts clad in red cedar weatherboards. Pulling Walt from her shoulder holster, Modeen sprinted to the barn door.

Spooky covered her six and then came in behind her. Flicking up her night vision goggles, she cracked the heavy door open, pushed it slightly ajar and peered inside.

The whole interior appeared to have been scrubbed until squeaky clean – or as clean as an old farm shed can be – and its painted concrete floor gave it a sterile look and feel. Portable floodlights were set up in each corner illuminating the central area, where plastic curtain 'walls' had been pulled aside to reveal an impressive collection of lab equipment.

The lights glinted off huge stainless steel boilers, settling tanks, separators, filtration units and a myriad of laboratory beakers, volumetric and Florence flasks and other paraphernalia, all sitting idle. Piles of boxes and packing material sat nearby and lab workers milled around, sorting and packing, as a gas forklift came and went, stacking boxed items and loading them onto the waiting semi.

Slipping inside and beneath the stairs leading to the turret, Modeen took cover behind a wall of large wooden crates. Spooky followed her in and pointed to a guard, armed with an M4 carbine, standing on a mezzanine floor at the far corner of the barn. They nodded to each other and holstered their pistols.

As they removed their side packs containing the C4 explosives, Spooky whispered, 'Set the timers for two minutes. I'll take the other side. We'll deploy the charges along the length, then come back through the middle and exit through here,' and he tilted his head at the door they'd just entered through. 'Time to make some noise.'

Unclipping his F90 rifle, he tucked it against his side. He used his free hand to shade his face as he sauntered across to the other side of the barn in clear view of anyone watching. Luckily the guard's focus was on the lab workers and tired forklift driver, who'd already managed to damage some expensive equipment in his haste to get the job done. Ducking in behind a large stainless steel storage tank, Spooky set his first charge.

After placing her first charge on the tower of crates she was hiding behind, Modeen moved quickly along the wall to the halfway point, where she slid the next charge under one of the boilers.

Unclipping the F90 machine gun from her webbing and setting it to auto, she shot out the floodlights behind and in front of her.

The two short bursts from the unsuppressed weapon jack-hammered throughout the building, followed by screams from the workers. Some sprinted for the exits while others scrambled to arm themselves. When Spooky shot out the remaining floodlights on his side of the barn, Modeen flipped her night vision goggles back down and watched as panic broke out in the sudden gloom.

Fleeing workers tumbled over equipment and clawed their way to the nearest exit. The forklift ploughed into a stack of boxes, while the guard on the mezzanine floor yelled and stumbled blindly toward the stairs. Modeen took him out with another quick burst from her F90, and then set her final charge.

She jogged to the staircase at the far end of the barn where Spooky was already waiting for her. Heading for the exit, they sprinted the full length of the barn, dodging stacked equipment and workers still stumbling about in the dark. One of the workers had unslung an AK47 and was staggering about, straining to see in the dimness. When he whipped around at the sound of their approach, Spooky dropped him with a short burst from his F90.

On the roof, the guard on the western turret had spun around on hearing the shots from inside. He pulled a Glock from his side holster and made to move toward the stairs when his body jerked and crimson and grey splattered against the wall to his left. His mouth fell open as his steps faltered and his body went limp. Falling against the railing, he tumbled over the balcony, hitting the ground four metres below.

Eight hundred metres away, there was a metallic click in the low vegetation as Bugs pulled back the bolt on the Vanquish Lapua Magnum. Expelling the used cartridge, he thrust it forward to feed a new round into the breech.

Calling through the comms, 'Exiting the eastern end of the barn,' to alert the watching snipers, Modeen came to a sliding stop at the door. Checking left and right, she headed out and toward the northern end of the grounds.

Hurdling the splayed body of another fallen guard, she and Spooky sprinted around the corner toward the bunker. Modeen strafed the occupant as they dove into the bunker and took cover, bracing themselves.

The sky lit up as a deafening BOOM erupted from the exploding barn. Fireballs burst from every opening and licked hungrily at the remaining weatherboards, while shards of metal and wood fell from the sky like rain. As a secondary blast flared, Modeen and Spooky looked away, shielding their eyes.

Observing a guard running from the fire, his mouth open, his body engulfed in a ball of flame and his arms waving frantically, Wolf ended his suffering with a single shot as Bugs' voice came over the comms.

'Four hostiles just ran out the back of the homestead into the side shed.' As he spoke, he noticed the curtains in a side window of the house being yanked aside. Seeing flashes from within and hearing loud pops, he hunkered down, crossing his arms and leaning low over the rifle to protect the scope.

Forty millimetre grenades hit the ground around him, exploding in clouds of dust and rock fragments.

At the same time, a Cherokee Jeep with a Maximi mounted on the back roof rack shot out of the shed, followed by two dirt bikes. The operator at the controls of the Maximi fought to keep his balance as the accelerating Jeep bounced around the back ring road. The high-powered two-stroke bikes peeled off to the left, jumped the windrow, and headed into the bush west of the compound.

Raising his head and spitting dust and grit out of his mouth, Bugs looked through the scope and coughed, 'Jeep … comin' down the western side.' Hastening to put the cross hairs on the Maximi operator, he let loose a hurried shot, but had to hunker down again as more grenades exploded around him, showering him in more rock fragments.

From their cover in the bunker, Modeen and Spooky had trained their weapons on the corner of the burning barn. The Cherokee surged into view, and then juddered and slowed as the driver's head exploded, splattering the windscreen.

The motor coughed, threatening to stall, as Modeen

and Spooky drilled the startled operator at the controls of the Maximi. He fell off the back of the vehicle, which gave a final chug and then rolled to a stop.

Pushing his mic closer to his mouth, Spooky whispered, 'Nice shot, Bugs.'

'Yeah, 'cept I was goin' for the guy on the Maximi.' Still hunkered down, Bugs coughed and spat. 'They've got a grenade launcher in the homestead and have made my position.' He coughed again. 'Any chance you could get 'em off me?'

Glancing around, he decided to retreat further back down the rocky outcrop. But as he made to move, the curtain on the next window in the homestead was yanked aside, and a high-powered machine gun strafed the top of the ridge he was behind.

'Oh man, I'm gettin' pounded here.'

'I can't see anything from this angle,' Wolf barked into the comms.

'I've got an idea.' Modeen patted Spooky on the back and rose to her feet. 'Cover me.' Sprinting out of the bunker, she flicked up her night vision goggles as the approaching daybreak and the glow from the burning barn rendered them redundant. She kept low and raced toward the Kenworth prime mover. Springing onto the running board, she yanked the door open and leapt inside.

Seconds later, Spooky heard the squeal as the air-starter engaged. This was followed by the throaty roar of a Cummins diesel engine. The Kenworth T909 B-double's prime mover bounced as it took up the weight of its partially loaded trailer and then surged forward.

Shifting, maximising the revs, toggling the splitter and double-clutching through the gears, Modeen accelerated hard around the ring road, using all of the Cummins' six hundred horse power. Skirting the stockyards, she swung right, lined up the rig with the back far corner of the homestead, and gave the roaring engine full throttle.

As she stormed toward the building, she saw a hefty man burst through the back door carrying an M4 carbine.

When he began firing at the charging rig, she merely stooped low in the driver's seat, stomped harder on the accelerator, and wrapped the seatbelt tighter around herself.

As it rammed head-on into the homestead, the Kenworth's huge bull bar obliterated the back porch. The force of the impact sent the house careering off its stumps, crumpling and disintegrating around the big rig as it continued to tear through the aged timber structure like a battering ram.

# CHAPTER SIXTEEN

The semi burst through the front corner of the shattered homestead, sending splinters and corrugated iron flying in all directions. From his position on the ridge, Wolf saw the big rig judder to a halt and sprang to his feet. Satisfied he and Bugs had neutralised the guards, he left the heavy AMR sniper rifle behind and dashed down the rocky slope, skidding in the scree as he gathered speed. Pulling the Glock from his shoulder holster, he sprinted toward what was left of the house.

Some eight hundred metres away, Bugs ducked as a helicopter swooped low over his head.

The agile two-seater R22 Robinson with glass bubble cockpit was a model popular for mustering work on large cattle stations. Glimpsing Reger at the stick with Foster at his side cradling a sniper rifle, Bugs swore under his breath.

The chopper hugged low over the terrain and then swivelled sideways in the air. Inside the cockpit Foster raised the SR98 bolt action, seven point six two calibre rifle to his shoulder and put his eye to the scope.

Reger flicked him a glance and barked, 'Wait.'

Foster scowled. 'I can get 'im from here. This thing's lethal up to eight hundred metres.'

'I said *wait.*'

On the ground, Wolf spotted the approaching helicopter and lengthened his stride as he raced toward the homestead.

With another drawn out, 'Waaiit,' Reger picked up a remote control from the chopper's console and threw Foster a sinister grin. Seeing Reger's thumb hovering over a button on the remote, Foster lowered the rifle and leered down at Wolf, who was running flat-out but was still several hundred metres from the homestead.

Throwing Foster a wink, Reger pressed the button. At the very same instant, a loud metallic sound resonated inside the cockpit and he found himself fighting to control the chopper. Below them, Bugs' triumphant smile dissolved into a look of horror as a triad of explosive charges erupted along the eastern perimeter of the property, swallowing a running Wolf in its destructive path.

Bugs' anguished bellow was lost amid the clamour of the chopper's death throes. It spun drunkenly in the air, black smoke billowing from its engine. Oblivious to everything else, Bugs broke cover and leapt to his feet.

As he took off at a sprint toward where he'd last seen Wolf, the chopper lost its fight for altitude. It plummeted to earth, engine screaming. Its rotors buckled as the fuselage slammed into the ground, and then the twisted wreckage burst into flames.


Stepping onto the Kenworth's running boards, Modeen climbed onto the bonnet and from there to the roof of the cab, where she squatted to view the carnage left in the semi's wake.

Just as she spied Spooky making his way toward her, a nearby noise caught her attention. Glancing to her right, she saw a large man climb out from amid the wreck of the house. Shoving away a sheet of roofing iron he staggered to his feet holding an AK47.

He shook his head, spat on the ground and then straightened to glance up at the semi. His eyes followed the trailer along to the cab and then it's roof. Stiffening, he went to raise his weapon only to give a sudden jolt and drop the rifle, before falling backward into the rubble. Modeen kept Walt trained on him and watched, but the man didn't move again. Satisfied he was no longer a threat, she lowered her pistol and surveyed the grounds of the homestead, noting the multiple prone bodies scattered around the yards.

*Wolf and Bugs have done their jobs well.*

Standing up, she looked toward the rocky ridge behind the south-eastern side of the property where she knew Wolf was stationed. Glimpsing the heli-copter's smoking carcass just beyond the ridge, her focus was suddenly drawn to a figure dashing through the bush on the south-western side of the road. Something about the figure's urgency gave her pause.

Pushing her mic closer to her mouth, she said, 'Bugs?' and heard him yell back, 'It's Wolf!'

Just two words, but they chilled her whole body.

Her anxious eyes scanned ahead of Bugs and focused on the settling cloud of red dust. Peering closer, she saw a prone black figure among the rocks.

With a gut-wrenching cry of, 'Wolf!' she leapt from the cab onto the bonnet then onto the collapsed roof of the house. From there she skidded down the corru-gated sheets to the ground and raced across the yard.

The hammering in her chest was not only due to exertion, and as her sprinting legs carried her across the ground, she murmured over and over through shaking lips, 'Please be alright … please be alive.'

Bugs reached Wolf first. Sprawled across a pile of rocks, his body was covered in rubble and dust. One arm was extended as though reaching for his Glock, which lay on the ground beside him. His left leg was bent at an unnatural angle beneath a boulder, and the side of his helmet was smashed and bloodied.

Squatting beside him, Bugs slung his med kit to the ground. Running assessing eyes over his mate's prone body, he carefully brushed away the rubble and was relieved to hear the big man give a grunt of pain.

'Don't try to move, mate.' He was checking Wolf's pulse when Modeen skidded to a halt beside them.

Dropping to her knees she bent low over Wolf, murmuring, 'Oh no … oh no.' She looked up at Bugs with anguished eyes, and he gave her shoulder a reassuring thump.

'He's alive.' Keeping a professional detachment in his tone, he continued. 'I'd say his left leg is broken, and there could be internal injuries….' He struggled to keep the anxiety out of his voice when he added, '… and head trauma.' Moving with purpose, he unslung the Falcon III AN/PRC handset from his pack and set up the small UHF Satcom antenna. 'Airborne Three, this is Ground Leader. We have a medical emergency and request immediate evac.'

'Copy Ground Leader. Are you under fire?'

'Negative Airborne Three. Hostiles have been neutralised.'

'Copy Ground Leader. ETA ten minutes.'

Hearing Wolf groan, Modeen began carefully loosening his kit, while Bugs examined the boulder trapping his leg. Rolling up his sleeves, he positioned himself to the side, wrapped his arms around the large rock, bunched his muscles, and heaved. As the weight was lifted from his leg, the semi-conscious Wolf gasped with pain, and Modeen's face crumpled.

Dropping the boulder to the side with a thud, Bugs straightened, wiping his brow, and threw her a pained glance. 'Had to do it.'

'I know.' To his ears, her voice sounded small and frightened, not at all like the Modeen he knew.

Bending to take a syrette out of the med kit and undoing the plastic cover, he said soothingly, 'I'll give him a Morphine jab, that'll help with the pain.'

A short time later Spooky's voice came across the comms. 'How is he?'

Bugs muttered, 'Unconscious, but alive.'

He and Modeen were working silently, splinting Wolf's leg when Spooky emerged from the spinifex. Coming to stand beside them, he put his hands on their shoulders and frowned down at his injured mate. After a few moments, he said quietly to Bugs, 'There's no sign of Reger or Foster.'

'Think you'll find they're in the downed chopper,' Bugs muttered through tight lips.

'Roger. I'll go check it.' With a final glance at Wolf, Spooky jogged away, toward the smoke trail on the hill.

'Oy!' Bugs called after him, 'Taipan will be here in ten.'


The R22 chopper's twisted fuselage hissed and creaked as smoke and steam issued from its cracked engine. Cautiously approaching the wreckage, Spooky eyed the shattered, stowed-in cockpit.

There was no one inside.

Taking the Glock from his shoulder holster, he bent

low, surveying the ground. Following a thin trail of blood leading away from the wreck he found Foster on the ground, propped against a large boulder. His breath came in agonised gasps, and his face and neck were slashed and bloodied, his left eye closed over. A sniper rifle lay across his lap, and he clutched his stomach with both hands as his body convulsed. Spitting up more blood, he blinked to clear the vision in his right eye and glanced up as Spooky came to stand in front of him.

Seeing thick arterial blood oozing from between Foster's fingers, Spooky lowered his weapon and said flatly, 'There's a chopper on the way.'

Foster tried to laugh, only to grimace and cough as his mouth filled with blood.

When Spooky barked, 'Where's Reger?' Foster's body convulsed again and he retched, spraying the front of his clothes and turning them a deeper shade of crimson.

Lifting a trembling hand, he wiped the dribble of blood from the side of his mouth and threw Spooky a defiant, one-eyed glare. Then, mustering his remaining energy, he reached for the rifle lying across his lap.

Spooky raised his Glock and shook his head. 'Don't.'

Foster ignored the warning. Gripping the handle, he lifted the rifle's muzzle.

Growling, 'Don't, Foster,' Spooky took a two-handed grip on his pistol and aimed it at Foster's head.

When the injured man merely sneered and made a herculean effort to aim the weapon, Spooky fired a single shot. The rifle clattered to the ground as Foster slumped back and then slid sideways down the boulder, coming to rest on the dusty ground with a neat hole in his forehead.

With a shake of his head, Spooky re-holstered his Glock and then turned to begin his search for more tracks. When he found a fresh set leading southward from the chopper toward the road, he announced over the comms, 'Foster's dead and Reger's on foot, headed south.'

'Copy that,' Bugs barked. 'Now get back here.'

Picking up the distant drone of a chopper, Spooky turned and jogged back to where the others waited with Wolf. He arrived to find the Taipan hovering above their heads as Wolf's stretcher was being winched into the chopper's cargo hold.

Glancing at Modeen, he noticed she'd donned a harness. As the winch cable came back down, Bugs grabbed the carabiner and clipped it onto the D-shackle at the front of her harness.

Leaning toward her, he yelled over the noise of the chopper, 'You stay with Wolf. Spook and I'll go after Reger. Then we'll do a sweep of the homestead and meet you back in Townsville.' At her nod he looked up, lifted a hand above his head, and gave the winch operator the thumbs-up.

Once safely in the cargo hold, Modeen gazed

silently down at the ground while the co-pilot unclipped the winch cable, stowed it away, and then helped her out of the harness. After watching Bugs and Spooky set off in the direction of the downed chopper, she turned to kneel at Wolf's side. Pressing her lips together to stop them quivering, she took one of his strong but now inert hands in hers.

Only vaguely aware of the co-pilot climbing into the cockpit, she heard him say to the pilot, 'Head injuries. We'd better get him to Townsville ASAP.'

Bugs and Spooky followed Reger's tracks for a distance until they arrived at the main gravel road that lead back to the homestead.

Stopping to squat on his haunches, Spooky murmured, 'Reger's tracks stop here.' He pointed to fresh tyre marks in the gravel. 'A car came in from the south and did a U-turn and picked him up.'

'Makes sense,' Bugs drawled, squatting beside him. 'I saw two vehicles leave the station during the mayhem, carrying three men and two women.' He shook his head. 'They were unarmed so we let them through.' Sighing, he rose, patting Spooky on the shoulder. 'May as well get back to the homestead and see if we can find any clues as to where they might go.'

'Right-o.'

As they jogged back along the road to the homestead, the sun broke over the eastern horizon, gilding the top of the fig tree in the wreckage-cluttered house yard.

Finding the barn still smouldering Bugs looked over at the semi, which stood tall amid the debris of the house, and gave a humourless grin. 'When did Modeen learn to drive a big rig?'

'I remember her tellin' me once she had an aunt who was a truck driver.'

'Oh yeah?' Bugs raised pale eyebrows as the two men continued walking toward the ruined homestead.

'Her parents lived in South Africa,' Spooky went on, 'but they used to send Modeen over here on school holidays to stay with her aunt, who'd often take her on long hauls all over the state.'

Bugs nodded. They walked in silence for a bit and then he said solemnly, 'I hope Wolf pulls through … for both their sakes.' Taking a fifty calibre Desert Eagle from his shoulder holster, he nudged Spooky. 'Come on mate, let's make sure there're no stragglers.'

———

The two male occupants of the black Ford sedan sat in silence as they cruised along the Flinders Highway toward Townsville. When his mobile phone chimed with an incoming text, the passenger said, 'We must be in mobile range now.' Clicking on the text message and quickly scanning it, he looked across at his companion. 'Wolf's been transferred to Brisbane hospital. He's in the ICU, in a coma.'

Bugs swore loudly and then sighed. 'You'd better give Ben a sit rep.'

Spooky nodded and tapped on Ben's number. The call was answered almost immediately.

'Report.' Ben's normally deep, controlled voice sounded strained.

'You know about Wolf?'

'Yes,' Ben barked, 'I'm at the hospital now and the doctors have filled me in on his condition. They're still running tests but it's not looking good. He's fallen into a coma and they're uncertain how long that will last, or...,' pausing, he said slowly, '... or if he'll come out of it at all.' Nobody spoke for a long moment and then Ben said flatly, 'I've informed the Feds about the lab at Julia Creek. They're on their way there to mop up.' He sighed and asked with a note of resignation in his voice, 'How'd you go with Reger?'

'He's still at large. I lost the trail south of the property, where a vehicle picked him up. From that point, he could've gone west to Cloncurry and Mt Isa, south to Winton, east toward Townsville, or anywhere in between.' Spooky's frustration was obvious while beside him, Bugs concentrated on the road.

'They'd just finished cooking a fresh batch of meths,' Spooky went on, 'and were about to relocate it and the whole lab to a new site when we dropped in.'

'Relocate it where?'

'Unsure. But we found a manifest in the big rig they were using to transport the stuff, a Kenworth semi they'd hired from Bluey's Haulage. According to the manifest, they were going to freight the cargo down south and store it at a warehouse in....' Taking the folded manifest out of a pocket, he read aloud, '... Cecil Hills, east of Sydney. From there, your guess is as good as mine as to where it was going. Looks like they only "dry hired" the rig.'

'So they were using their own driver?'

'Yep. I guess they needed the bigger truck to move all the equipment in the lab at once.'

'Anything else?'

'Yeah, the hire was pre-paid by the Davidson Family Trust.'

'Well, we don't have to worry about Davidson or Bellamy anymore, the Feds have them both in custody.' A hopeful note crept into Ben's voice. 'Did you come up with any other leads?'

'We searched through the remains of the homestead – you heard what happened to it?'

'I did.'

'We also searched the bodies of the guards and found a computer print-out in the pocket of one of them. It appears the black Ford sedans they were using were all hired from Alpha One car hire in Brisbane, and paid for online by Rotorua Holdings Propriety Limited.'

Ben exhaled. 'That makes sense, considering who's involved.'

'Bugs and I are on our way back to Townsville. I

assume you want us to catch the next available flight to Brisbane?'

'Affirmative.'

About to hang up, Spooky paused. 'How's Modeen holding up?'

'She hasn't left his side.'

Spooky frowned at the thread of concern in Ben's voice. 'That's no surprise, is it?'

'Of course not,' Ben said brusquely. 'It's just … worrying that she's so quiet and withdrawn.'

# CHAPTER SEVENTEEN

The soles of Ben's black business shoes squeaked on the scrubbed tiles as he strode along the brightly-lit corridor toward the intensive care unit. Along the way he passed scurrying nursing staff and was himself passed by the occasional trolley-pushing wards man or MD rushing toward the next emergency.

Just another busy day at Brisbane Hospital.

As he neared the end of the corridor Ben slowed and stopped outside a room. Standing in the doorway, he gazed silently inside. Under the dimmed lights Wolf lay motionless on the bed, a pulse oximeter attached to one finger to measure the oxygen in his blood, and a broad tube down his windpipe connected to a nearby ventilator. By the bedhead an electronic monitor blinked, recording his heart and respiratory rate.

When Ben stepped into the room, where the only sounds were the hums and soft beeps of the monitoring equipment, he glimpsed Modeen on the opposite side of the bed.

Still in her black tactical gear she sat silent and unmoving in a chair, elbows on her knees and head in her hands. Hearing his approach she glanced up, and he gave a small nod of greeting as he moved to the bedside and gazed down at Wolf.

Dragging a hand through her hair, still gritty with Julia Creek dust, she said wearily, 'The doctors have done CT scans and EEG tests, trying to get a more accurate idea of his condition.' She swallowed. 'We should know more tomorrow.'

Ben came around the bed to kneel beside her chair and take her hands in his. In his large, warm grip, her hands felt small and chilled. 'Why don't you take a break and get some rest, JD? The medical staff will look after Wolf, and I'll keep you posted on any change in his condition.'

Seeing the compassion in his dark eyes, Modeen's own eyes filled with tears. Gently removing a hand from his grasp, she reached up to pull a chain out from beneath the front of her shirt. A gold ring dangled from the chain and glinted under the light.

She rubbed the ring reverently between her thumb and fingers and said tearfully, 'Troy, he … he asked me to marry him, Ben. He … wanted this to be our last mission.' A fat tear breached her lids to slide unchecked down her cheek. 'W-why did this have to happen n-now?' Her voice broke as a sob caught in her throat.

Ben pulled her to him and wrapped his arms around her. Burying her face in his broad chest, she gave release to the tears she'd been keeping at bay. He let her cry, holding her as her body was wracked with sobs. When her weeping lessened and she drew back, sniffing and dragging the back of a hand across her eyes, he kept hold of her arms.

'Wolf's one tough soldier, and he's going to pull through.' Bending his head, he gazed into her red-rimmed eyes. 'You know that, don't you.' He stated it as a fact, not a question. She gave a teary nod as he helped her up from the chair. 'Come on, I'll get you squared away.'

'I have to stay close—'

'Don't worry, I've organised some accommodation for you nearby. After I drop you there, I'll come back and stay with him.'

———

At twenty-one hundred Spooky and Bugs strode into the ICU ward. They moved with purpose, Spooky carrying a case and Bugs with a duffel over a broad shoulder, a muscular arm holding it firmly in place. Still in jackboots and black combat fatigues, and with grim faces smudged in outback dust, they stood out against the sterile brightness of the ward and the white or pale blue scrubs of the medical staff, some of whom gaped at them as they went past. After checking with the wide-eyed ward nurse, they headed to Wolf's room and were greeted by Ben and a showered and rested Modeen.

Glancing around to make sure they were alone, Bugs slung the duffel from off his shoulder and handed it to Modeen, while Spooky passed her the aluminium case, saying, 'I believe these are yours.'

She took them without speaking and all four gazed at Wolf.

After a few moments Bugs asked in a gravelly voice, 'How's the big fella travellin'?'

In answer, Modeen and Ben stepped aside so the others could move closer to the bed. They gazed down at Wolf, still lying motionless but now with two additional tube attachments, one to his skull and the other inserted up a nostril. In response to a watchful Ben's brusque query, the owl-eyed nurse attaching them had explained, rather breathlessly, that the tube connected to Wolf's skull measured and relieved any intracranial pressure, while the nasogastric tube prevented aspiration of gastric contents into his lungs.

Nobody spoke for a long moment and then Bugs piped up, trying to lighten the mood, 'Wow. He's a mad Trekky you know, and told me once he wanted to be part Borg. When he's all better, he'll be glad to hear he actually looked like one for a while. Maybe I'll take a photo for his scrap book.'

Glancing at Modeen, Spooky noticed a red puffiness around her eyes and said gently, 'He's one tough hombre, he won't let this beat him.'

The others nodded and murmured their agreement as Ben announced, 'There's a common room at the end of the hallway. Let's go grab a coffee.'

They sat in companionable silence, sipping their machine-dispensed coffees, immersed in their thoughts. Spooky broke the contemplative silence to bring Modeen up to speed with events following the chopper evac. He kept his voice low and checked regularly for anyone within hearing range, and when he'd finished, Ben spoke up.

'The hire of the B-Double looks legit. John O'Shea, or Bluey of Bluey's Haulage, checked out clean.' He glanced at Spooky. 'As you know, Bluey wasn't their usual operator, and they only dry-hired the rig. They made sure to give him a 'tight-lips' bonus if he kept things on the quiet. I managed to get him talking, though.'

The others shared a half grin, well aware of how convincing their boss, old CO, and VC recipient, Ben Logan, could be.

'His insurance should cover the damages to the rig.' As he spoke, Ben gave Modeen a sideways glance.

Bugs threw her a wink over the lip of his coffee cup. 'Have to say, Modeen, that was an impressive bit of improvisation. You saved my butt back there, thanks mate.'

Ben went on, his voice composed and his words clipped. 'I want to thank each one of you for your hard work and expertise. This morning you successfully disrupted one of the biggest meth lab operations in the state.' He looked at each of them in turn. 'I know how you're feeling about Wolf … I feel the same way.'

At his words, the others lowered their heads to gaze at the floor, and Modeen swiped an impatient hand across her eyes.

'And I feel like that about every one of you,' Ben went on. 'Dealing with critically wounded team members never gets any easier, but being injured is one of the risks we take for our nation's security.' He paused. 'And on that basis, I've been advised by HQ that Reger has been deemed a risk to national security.' When the others looked up at him again, Ben lifted his chin. 'And as such, he is to be actively pursued.'

Spooky frowned. 'Pursued?'

Ben met his gaze dispassionately. 'I'll be sending you and Bugs an event number. Reger is to be found … and if necessary, neutralised.'

Bugs gave a curt nod of his dusty, buzz-cut head. 'Right, so where do we start?'

'With Rotorua Holdings Propriety Limited, given Reger's association with the Black Mamba organisation. And what we know about Rotorua Holdings' connection with the hire cars used in Olman's hit.

Apart from their New Zealand undertakings, RHPL operates under a number of trading names, three of which are nightclub operations, in Melbourne, Perth, and Kings Cross in Sydney. They also own a string of minor hotels dotted around Australia. I'll email you the addresses and GPS coordinates for each of those businesses.

'For now, I want you to arrange a hire car and head down to Sydney, where I'll organise for a NatSec vehicle to be waiting for you. Then you can begin working your way through the list, followed by Melbourne and then Perth.'

'What if we uncover further illicit operations during the pursuit?'

'We'll assess that on a case-by-case basis, Spook. And I'll pass on any other intel I get on Reger's where-abouts as it's received.'

Modeen had been staring at Ben the whole time he'd been speaking. Now, when he paused, she asked quietly, 'What about me?'

Turning to the other two, he said, 'Can you give us a minute?'

'Sure. C'mon, Spook, lets go tell Wolf some jokes.' Bugs grinned. 'Maybe we can wake 'im up.'

'We'll meet you back at the room,' Ben called after them, before turning to Modeen. He regarded her levelly and then said, 'JD, as of now you're on four weeks inactive duty.'

Her lips tightened.

*I knew it.*

Seeing her open her mouth to protest, he raised a halting hand. 'Bugs and Spooky can drop you home in the hire car.'

'I can make my own way—'

Ben raised a hand again. 'I want them breaking the journey in any case, and the Gold Coast is on the way.'

Modeen frowned and straightened to sit stiffly upright in her chair, as Ben went on sombrely, 'Wolf could be in ICU for months.' He dragged a hand over his dark head. 'As you know, his next of kin are all in Tasmania. I contacted his brother Jake, who told me their widowed mother has been diagnosed with Alzheimer's. She's now in an aged care facility.'

He paused, eyeing her. 'Jake said Wolf had told him about you....' Seeing her bite her lip as tears welled in her eyes again, he hurried on. 'In light of Jake's other responsibilities, and because he knew it'd be what his brother would want, Jake suggested Wolf stay here in Queensland, where he'll be close to you. Jake and his wife will fly up and visit whenever they can.'

When Modeen remained tight-lipped, staring at the floor, Ben sighed.

'Of course I'll need to run this past him first, but I doubt Jake would have any reservations about Wolf being transferred to the Gold Coast Hospital, where it'll be more convenient for you.' Getting to his feet, Ben extended a hand. 'Think about it. I don't expect an answer right away, I know you've got a lot on your plate at the moment.'

Without speaking, she took his hand and rose to face him.

Taking a business card from the inside pocket of his suit he said gently, 'You're not alone in this. If you need to talk, you can call me anytime. Or you can contact the people on this number,' and he handed her the card. 'They're professional counsellors, JD, and you can trust them to keep confidential any discussions you have.'

———

With all three immersed in thoughts of their comatose mate, the drive to Surfers Paradise was spent in quiet contemplation. When, at around midnight, they pulled into a parking bay out the front of Modeen's apartment building, she broke her silence to bid them farewell and urge them to take care.

'You too, Modeen,' Spooky said, giving her a hug. 'You want me to see you to your door?'

'Nah, I'll be alright … but thanks.' A sudden thought occurred to her. 'Where are you guys staying? I've got plenty of room if you'd like to bunk here.'

'It's OK,' Bugs called from the driver's seat. 'Leanne's booked us into an apartment at the Southport Meriton. It's a two bedroom unit, so I won't have to suffer Spooky's snoring.'

Ignoring the teasing jibe, Spooky added, 'And we

leave for Sydney early tomorrow morning. Wouldn't want to disturb you by stomping around in the wee hours.' He gave her arm a final squeeze before climbing back into the passenger seat.

'Seeya Modeen,' Bugs called. 'Look after y'self. Tell Wolf we're thinkin' of 'im, and that I'll have some more jokes to tell next time we see 'im.'

Nodding and pressing her lips together, Modeen watched as they drove away.

When their taillights disappeared around a corner, she turned and made her way slowly into the building. Stepping into the lift, she found herself alone for the first time in days. With that awareness came a crushing sensation of bereavement, and a sudden chill as fears flooded in. Her mind filled with images of Wolf, motionless as a cadaver on the bed, tubes connecting him to cold, blinking machines ... machines that were helping keep him alive.

She sucked in a shuddering breath and squeezed her eyes tightly closed, wishing she'd stayed at the hospital where regular distractions kept her worst fears at bay. When the lift doors swished open on the top floor she bolted out, grateful to escape the confines of both the elevator and her own internal terrors.

Making her way along the corridor, she let herself into her penthouse apartment where she was greeted with a drift of Chanel No5 from the main guest room. Blinking, she felt a rush of comfort.

*Aunty Hann must still be here.*

Her inner chill receded somewhat and her shoulders relaxed. She gave a grateful sigh, and then spotted two empty wine glasses on the sink.

*And she's had company.*

Heading to her room, she dropped her metal case and duffel in a corner and made straight for the ensuite. Standing under the rain shower, she lifted her face to let the water wash over it and down her body. Rolling her shoulders, she lent her hands against the tiles as the water coursed down her neck and back, easing both her weary muscles and her anxious mind. A short time later, dressed in singlet and boy-leg panties, she slipped beneath the sheets and was almost instantly asleep.

Thankfully, she was too tired to dream.

She awoke to laughter coming from the kitchen. Her aunt's laugh was easily recognisable, as was the male voice accompanying it. Intrigued, she threw back the bedclothes and sat up. Who would both she and her aunt know here in Surfers Paradise? After first making a quick call to the hospital to be told Wolf's condition was stable, she pulled on tracksuit bottoms and a T-shirt, all the while telling herself to stay positive.

*No change to his condition also means it hasn't worsened.*

When she wandered out to the kitchen, she found her aunt standing at the sink and a man sitting at the breakfast bar with his back to Modeen. He had a steaming mug in front of him and was dressed casually in jeans and short-sleeved shirt. Still in her dressing gown, Hannah was spreading butter on slices of toast. Chatting happily, she glanced up and her eyes fell on her niece.

'Morning, Aunty Hann.' Her aunt's smile widened with pleased surprise as she hurried around the counter to hug Modeen warmly.

'Josephine! We didn't hear you arrive home last night, love.'

'Yeah, it was late.' As she spoke, Modeen threw the man a small smile. 'And morning to you too, Salty.'

Dipping his head, Richard Salt returned her smile, as a clearly flustered Hannah exclaimed, 'Oh yes! I hope you don't mind my inviting Richard to stay over. I met him at the conference. He's another budding author, you know.'

Modeen peered at a grinning Salty. 'Did Ben ask you to keep an eye on me?'

Salty frowned, appearing genuinely surprised. 'No, youngster. It's like your delightful aunt said,' at which Hannah gave a coquettish titter, 'we met at the confer-ence. And when there was a double-booking issue at my accommodation, she kindly offered to let me stay here.'

He peered at her, noting a new puffiness around her eyes. 'And why would you, of all people, need looking after?'

Despite her best efforts, Modeen's face crumpled. Putting an arm around her, Hannah said soothingly, 'Come on, love, how about you sit down and tell us what happened.'

Pulling out the kitchen stool beside Salty, Hannah waited until Modeen was seated before settling herself on the next stool along.

Blinking, Modeen took a deep breath to calm herself. 'One of the soldiers in my unit was … critically injured. He's in a coma.'

'Oh love, that's awful.' Hannah cupped Modeen's cheek in a warm hand, while on her other side Salty squeezed her shoulder.

'Sorry to hear that, Jo,' he said gently. 'Anyone I know?'

Biting back a sob, Modeen murmured, 'W-wolf.'

Hearing Salty's sudden intake of breath, Hannah threw him a frown and then jumped down from her stool. 'How about I make you a cuppa, love?' she said brightly, 'and some brekkie.'

While Hannah bustled around in the kitchen boiling the jug, rattling crockery and cutlery, Salty leaned closer to Modeen and whispered, 'What happened?'

With a sideways glance at him, she muttered, 'Hasn't Ben briefed you?'

He sat back. 'Honestly, Jo, my being here is by pure coincidence. I had no idea you and Hannah were related, she just said she was staying with her favourite niece. When we got talking some more, and I saw the photos around the place, I twigged. And of course now that I see you together, there's an obvious resemblance.'

'So you're telling me you're attending a writer's conference for *real?*'

He gave a shy grin. 'I am. And Hannah and I met at the sessions on writing memoirs.'

It was Modeen's turn to grin. 'Wow. Both your memoirs will be worthwhile reads.'

Just then Hannah carried over a mug of coffee and placed it in front of her. 'While your toast's cooking, I'll just pop in and get dressed. We'll have to go shortly.' She frowned. 'Unless you want me to stay here with you, love?'

'Of course not, Aunty Hann. You go, I'll be fine.'

'Well … if you're sure?'

Modeen smiled. 'I'm sure.'

As Hannah toddled off to her room, Salty said quietly, 'So what happened to Wolf?'

Modeen sighed and bent her head. 'We were on a mission out west and raided a meth lab. Wolf was … caught up in an explosion.'

'Oh.' He paused and then murmured, 'I hope he'll be OK.'

'You and me both.' Lifting her chin, she nudged him with an elbow. 'And now I'd like to know what your intentions are toward my aunt?'

He gave an amused snort and his eyebrows twitched. 'Nothing untoward, I assure you.'

'Just as long as you remember whose aunt she is.'

This time he laughed openly. 'As if I'd be likely to forget that!' After watching her take a long drink of coffee, his expression grew sombre. 'Seriously, Jo, do you need any help? You know I can be trusted.'

'Of course I know that.' Regarding him levelly, she exhaled through pursed lips. 'It's a long story, but basically I was tasked to protect the premier....' She frowned into her mug. 'And you know how that turned out.'

He nodded. 'It's been in the papers and on the news. A gang called The Black Mambas is meant to be behind the hit.'

'That's right, but it's more complicated than that, and has links to the past we didn't foresee.' She took another mouthful of coffee and checked her aunt's door was still closed. 'Remember the guy responsible for taking Ben's wife hostage? And before that, for kidnapping my father?'

'Yeah, Gator. How could I forget? You don't mean *he's* involved in this? After all, isn't he—'

She frowned. 'Yes, he's dead. But two of his close associates, John Reger and Jackson Foster, are also associated with the Black Mambas and have terrorist ties. They—'

'Reger?' Salty cut in. 'Now there's a name I've heard before in connection with criminal activities.'

'Yeah?'

'Mm.' He spoke slowly, recalling. 'I had dealings with one Thomas Reger, a fine upstanding citizen … at first. A highly decorated soldier if I remember right. Served in New Guinea during WWII and managed to survive the conflict and the miserable, disease-ridden conditions to return home to West Oz. He bought a farm in Yarloop, south of Perth, and started a tree milling business. Worked hard and did well for himself too, 'til hard times hit, and the government he'd risked his life for, abandoned him.'

Modeen shook her head sadly as Salty went on.

'He couldn't bear the thought of greedy creditors moving in to pick over everything he'd worked long and hard for, so being a resourceful beggar, Reger turned his hand to illicit ventures in order to keep the farm afloat. And that's when our paths crossed. He was one cagey operator, though, he didn't make things easy for me. But I finally pinned something on him … something that stuck. And when he was incarcerated, his sons inherited the farm and, I assume, all his legal and not-so-legal business interests.' Salty eyed her gravely. 'If this Jon Reger is one of Thomas's relations – his son even – I can only imagine you had a fight and a half on your hands.'

She sighed. 'We successfully shut down the operation, but Reger escaped. Ben has sent Bugs and Spooky after him.'

'I see.' About to say more, Salty stopped on seeing Hannah emerge from the guest bedroom.

'You'd better get dressed, Richard,' she called, 'or we'll miss the first information session.'

Standing to attention and throwing Modeen a wink, Salty saluted and barked, 'Yes ma'am.'

# CHAPTER EIGHTEEN

With her house guests in their rooms getting ready to leave, a sense of quiet descended on the apartment. To Modeen it was a brooding quiet, like the stillness that settles around a crouching predator.

She stood in the ensuite, both hands on the edge of the marble vanity, head bowed and eyes closed, breathing in and out while mulling things over. She stayed that way a long time, playing out various scenarios in her mind.

And each ended unsatisfactorily … except for one.

Slowly raising her head, she stared at her reflection in the mirror. At the frustration and desperate sorrow she saw there, her expression hardened and she banged both fists on the vanity. This time when she glared into her own eyes, she saw a grim determination in their blueness. Leaning down, she took a first aid kit out of the middle drawer and zipped it open.

Impatiently shoving aside the rolled bandages, she grasped a small scalpel.

Taking a wider stance in front of the mirror, she bent her right arm behind her head and gripped the back of her shirt. Wielding the scalpel in her left hand, she clenched her teeth and reached across to make a small incision in the soft inner skin just below the firm bicep of her right arm. Wincing, she dropped the bloodied scalpel into the basin and then, using her thumb and index finger, worked the tissue around the incision until a small metal cylinder protruded through the opening.

Grabbing a pair of tweezers from out of the kit, she gripped the cylinder and yanked it out.

She raised it to her face and stared thoughtfully at it for a moment, before rinsing it under the faucet and setting it down on the vanity counter. She took a swab from the kit and used it to mop up the blood around the incision. Keeping her right arm raised, she opened another drawer and fumbled around until her fingers found a small tube of super glue. Once satisfied she'd removed most of the blood, she applied a small drop of the glue to the incision and pinched the edges together. She sucked in a pained breath as a knock came on her bedroom door.

'Josephine love? We're heading off.'

Glancing at the cylinder on the vanity, she grabbed it and called, 'Just a sec, Auntie Hann.' Hastily pulling down the sleeve of her shirt to cover the fresh wound, she raced to the door.

Outside, wearing a floral maxi-dress cinched with a red belt above matching shoes, and holding a red handbag, Hannah stood smiling up at her. Behind her, Salty, now dressed in chinos and collared shirt, stood waiting in the living room.

'I won't be home when you return, Aunty Hann. I'm going back to Brisbane Hospital to be with Troy.'

'Oh right, of course, dear.'

Pulling her aunt in close for a hug, Modeen glanced down at her red handbag and found what she was looking for – a small gap at the end of the bag's zipper. With one quick, smooth movement, she dropped the cylinder through the gap and watched it disappear into the bulging bag's plentiful contents.

Drawing back, she held Hannah at arm's length, smiling warmly. 'Feel free to stay on here as long as you like. I'll be away for a while … at least a few days.' She glanced at Salty and found him eyeing her. 'And that goes for you too, Salty.'

His face split into a wide grin. 'Why, that's mighty kind of you, youngster.'

'Thanks, love.' Hannah gave her a final peck on the cheek and then stood back to gaze at her in concern. 'Now … are you gonna be OK?'

'Yep, I'll be fine.'

'Well … just look after yourself.'

'I will. Now off you go or you'll be late.'

As the door swung shut behind them, Modeen sprang into action. Moving deftly, she turned on her computer and began re-packing her duffel while the laptop booted up.

Taking out her NatSec phone, she removed the battery and tucked the mobile among the lingerie in a dresser drawer. When her gaze fell on the aluminium case in the corner of her bedroom she gave a regretful sigh, knowing she'd have to leave it behind.

Sitting in front of her laptop, she called up an airline booking site and compared flights out of Coolangatta airport to those from Brisbane. It took her less than a minute to decide it would be quicker to drive to Brisbane and catch a flight from there. Pressing the Enter key, she watched the printer on her desk in the corner of the lounge spit out a boarding pass.

Back in her bedroom, she changed into a pair of blue jeans and white T-shirt. Slinging her duffel over a shoulder, she let herself out of the apartment and made her way to the building's basement, where her dark blue Kawasaki GTR 1400 motorcycle sat patiently waiting.

Strapping the duffel across the back seat, she clicked open the near pannier and removed her full-face Shoei helmet.

Giving it a quick swipe of her hand to remove any dust, she slipped the helmet over her blonde head.

When she turned the key in the ignition, the big bike started straight away as though poised and eager for the opportunity to stretch its legs. Once out on the M1 freeway, with its rider tucked neatly behind the faring, it sailed effortlessly toward Brisbane at one hundred and ten kilometres an hour.

Taking the Gateway exit, Modeen arrived at the airport in good time. After securing the bike in the long-term parking, she strode into the terminal building as the first call for passengers to board the flight to Perth came over the loud speakers.

She dozed fitfully during the first leg of the flight, and had to hold her impatience in check during the brief stop-over in Adelaide. And when the Qantas flight took off for the final leg to Perth, she was wide awake.

And stayed that way.


Making her way to the line of hire car booths at the airport, she found one that had a mid-sized sedan available and promptly hired it.

At seventeen hundred hours she drove away from Perth's domestic airport in a silver-grey Hyundai Sonata. After turning left onto the Great Eastern High-way, she took the Tonkin Highway exit and headed south. The car's on-board GPS advised that the time to her destination was seventy-five minutes, and urged her to take a right onto the Roe Highway at Forrest-field, the quickest route.

It was getting dark by the time she hit Ravenswood,

where she turned onto Pinjarra Road which connected to the South Western Highway.

*Next stop, Yarloop.*

At that time of day the little town was deserted, not another car, person or even stray dog within sight. In the main street, she slowed the car to a crawl as she passed the general store and post office, both of which were closed up and dark. When lights ahead caught her eye she accelerated and headed that way, and found herself outside the Yarloop Hotel.

She pulled into one of the numerous empty parking bays outside the lowset building, which to her looked more like a tavern than a hotel, but she wasn't about to argue that point with the publican.

Behind the bar a hard-faced woman in her sixties turned on hearing Modeen enter. She wore a short, tight dress with a plunging neckline and what had to be a push-up bra beneath it – both two sizes too small – and had bottle-black curly hair above a face so heavily plastered in makeup it could've been applied with a shovel. She eyed Modeen up and down, making no attempt to greet her. The only other occupants were an elderly man at the end of the bar, and what appeared to be a young woman sitting in a dimly-lit corner wearing a Che Guevara T-shirt and cargo pants.

Pasting a smile on her face, Modeen asked politely,

'Sorry to bother you, but would you know where the Reger farm is? I'm looking for Jon Reger.'

The lady publican raised an over-plucked and thinly pencilled-back-in eyebrow and drawled in a gravelly smoker's voice, 'You drinkin?'

Modeen eyed her and then took out her wallet. 'Scotch and dry, thanks.' She dropped a ten dollar note on the bar as she spoke.

Seeing that, the barmaid's expression softened a tad. 'Johnny Walker Red?'

At Modeen's nod, the woman poured the drink and then put it on the bar in front of her, splashing some of it onto the grotty and already soaked towelling bar runner. Fixing Modeen with beady eyes, she said, 'So you're lookin' for the Reger place. Who wants to know?'

Modeen pulled up a bar stool and took a sip of her drink before answering. 'An old Army buddy of his.'

Thrusting both hands on her wide hips and throwing her head back, the woman gave a harsh laugh. 'Hah! Reger was in the special forces, 'n far as I know, there ain't no women at that level.' Her lips twisted with sour envy. ''Specially women that look like *you*.'

Modeen raised an amused eyebrow. 'Actually, he wasn't even a Commando.' Lifting the glass to her lips again, she said sweetly, 'He didn't have the aptitude or dedication to get into the Special Air Services Regiment … apparently.'

The woman's lips with their over-generous coating of crimson lipstick tilted further downward and she turned away, huffing, 'The Reger farm's twelve clicks down Johnston Road, first turn left after you cross Regers Creek. Can't miss the old homestead.'

'Thank you.' Not bothering to finish her drink, Modeen got down from the stool and headed to the door.

Once outside she pulled out her personal mobile, clicked on the Maps app and strode over to the Hyundai, typing in Johnston Road as she went. After studying the map for a few moments, she glanced up the street, realising she'd passed the road on her way into town. Climbing into the driver's seat, she nosed the hire car out of the parking bay and drove back past the post office and general store, and out onto the highway.

Inside the Yarloop Hotel, the woman in the corner had watched Modeen leave. Rising to her feet she hurried to the back door, flicking a fifty dollar note onto the bar as she went. Snatching up the note, the barmaid promptly tucked it into her bra and began hassling the old drunk to leave so she could lock up for the night.

Once outside, the woman jogged to where a late model Toyota Hilux was parked against the side of the hotel. She wasted no time climbing aboard the 4WD utility, which sported extra-wide all-terrain tyres, beefed-up suspension and a heavy duty bull-bar.

Putting her mobile phone to her ear, the woman started the car, backed it up, and then roared away with a spray of gravel.

Turning into Johnston Road, Modeen zeroed the odometer before accelerating to the nominated speed limit of a hundred kph. As she sped along the narrow, single lane bitumen track, she kept an eye on the odometer, and was just looking up from it when something grey flashed in the glare of her headlights. When it rocketed across the road in front of the car, she touched the brakes and swerved, barely missing the kangaroo. The Hyundai, perfectly adequate as far as sedans go but not a performance car by any stretch, responded by sliding its rear end into the gravel and then fishtailing when Modeen accelerated hard to flick the car back onto the road.

After that close encounter she continued more cautiously, keeping her speed to a more manageable seventy kph, which also allowed her to take in the surroundings. In the glow of her headlights she could see the bush on either side of the road was sparsely dotted with blackboys and acacia trees, and apart from the wildlife she'd encountered, she didn't see another soul on the lonely stretch of road.

When the odometer signalled she'd reached the twelve kilometre mark, the car's lights picked up a gentle rise in the road where denser, more lush vegetation hugged the edge. The car thumped over what felt like deep ruts.

*I guess that was Regers Creek.*

Keeping an eye out for the first road to her left, she went past a wide gravel track and skidded to a stop.

*Could that be the road?*

She backed up and turned down the track, which wound its way to the right. When she glimpsed a light in the distance, she switched off the headlights and slowed the car to a crawl.

*I could put on my night vision goggles….*

But as her eyes adjusted to the low light, she realised she could see quite well enough in the silver glow of the half moon. After following the track for about two hundred metres, she caught a glimpse of the homestead on a rise, just before the track turned sharply to the right and a gate loomed out of the dark in front of the Hyundai.

The faded sign hanging crookedly on the gate said 'Reger'.

Reversing up to the rise again, Modeen reached behind to the back seat and opened her duffel. Not wanting to give her position away, she kept the interior light off as she felt around and pulled out a pair of military binoculars. Buzzing the driver's side window down and putting the binoculars to her eyes, she surveyed the house and checked its range. The place and yard looked quiet, and the range finder indicated one hundred and two metres to the homestead.

Taking off her white T-shirt, she dug a black one out of her duffel and pulled it over her head. She also kicked off her joggers, exchanging them for jackboots. Feeling around in her duffel once more, she came across a set of car keys.

*For my NatSec vehicle. Damn, I didn't mean to bring them from home.*

She paused and then smiled to herself.

*Although ... they might come in handy.*

Pocketing the keys, she was about to get out of the Hyundai when she heard a nearby engine rev as it was changed down a gear and then gunned.

*Another vehicle, approaching fast.*

With a quick glance in the rear view mirror, she sucked in a breath and braced herself as a bull-bar materialised out of the darkness and the large vehicle it was attached to bore down on her.

When it slammed into the hire car, the force of the impact thrust her back in her seat as the stationary Hyundai's rear end was thrown into the air and the car pushed diagonally across the road. Its rear wheels came back to earth with a thud as it skidded into the shallow gutter along the road edge. It came to rest with its boot badly stowed in, passenger side toward the gutter, and driver's side rear wheel off the ground.

Still in the driver's seat, Modeen raised her head above the door's sill to locate her attacker as the other vehicle's lights blazed on and into her eyes. When two quick shots from a nine millimetre pistol shattered her window, missing her head by millimetres, she unclipped her seatbelt and dropped to the floor. Moving across to the passenger's side, she opened the door and slipped into the gutter.

Taking the NatSec car keys from her pocket, she squeezed both sides of the remote until a section detached from the base. As she carefully removed that section from the main one still containing the keys, she heard the other car's door close and footsteps crunch over the gravel toward her. When she raised her head again, another two shots whizzed past.

The footsteps were getting closer. When she judged them to be five metres away, she pressed the lock button on the detached segment of the remote. The red LED on it flashed, and she threw it toward the approaching footsteps. Bending low, she covered her ears.

And three seconds later an explosion shook the badly damaged Hyundai, showering it and the surrounding area in gravel and dust.

# CHAPTER NINETEEN

Coughing and shaking off dust and bits of gravel, Modeen stuck her head out from behind the Hyundai to survey the immediate area.

*If the explosion didn't kill my attacker, hopefully it disorientated him enough for me to get the upper hand.*

Shading her eyes from the other vehicle's headlights, she scanned for movement.

There was none that she could see.

Keeping low, she broke cover and moved toward the other vehicle, her senses on high alert for any kind of activity. Glancing across at the homestead, thinking the blast would've alerted anyone inside, she picked up no movement or sound from that direction either. She stumbled when her foot found a plate-sized divot in the road surface where the remote had detonated, and she looked back at the Hyundai. Its dust-covered duco was peppered all over by tiny dents like hail damage.

Her assailant's vehicle, a 4WD Toyota utility, was still idling nearby. She crept past it to scan the area from behind its headlights.

Nothing.

The driver's side door was slightly ajar. Reefing it open, she climbed in and reversed the heavy vehicle slowly backward, turning the wheel so the headlights panned past the Hyundai to highlight a wider area.

*There!*

Putting the Toyota into neutral, she yanked on the hand brake and rested her forearms on the steering wheel, staring at a dark mass on the ground about ten metres away. It lay in the gutter on the opposite side of the road from the Hyundai. When it remained completely still, she got out of the ute, still eyeing the mound, and approached cautiously. Shadows cast by foliage in front of the headlights made it hard to confirm what the mass was until she was almost on top of it.

The body of a woman, limbs splayed and face down in the gutter.

When Modeen rolled her over, the image of Che Guevara stared defiantly up at her, his face splattered with blood and caked in a fine layer of dust. Sitting back on her heels, she gazed at the dead woman and gave a slow nod of her head.

*From the Yarloop Hotel.*

Moving closer, she kneeled beside the body to check the pockets.

*Nothing … her gun must be somewhere close by.*

As she ran both hands down the sides of the woman's blood-stained cargo pants, she realised the left leg ended in a ragged, meaty stump just below the knee.

*She must've stepped on the IED.*

Feeling around, hoping to find the pistol, Modeen came up with nothing. Rolling the body over again, she found a canvas wallet and a hotel room key in a back pocket. With a satisfied grunt she rose to her feet and walked toward the ute to inspect the objects in the glow of the vehicle's headlights. The wallet, obviously made from hemp, boldly displayed a marijuana leaf on the front. Opening it, she found a driver's licence with the name Leila Mazlin on it. Seeing the photo of an attractive, dark-haired woman staring back at her with a mix of insolence and challenge in her eyes, Modeen glanced over at the motionless dark mass.

*So that's who you were and what you looked like, Leila Mazlin.*

Staring down at the licence again she noted the date of birth, 1983.

*And you were thirty-two years old.*

Holding the hotel key up to the light, she saw the Lord Forrest Hotel's name inscribed on it along with a Bunbury address, and beneath that, ROOM 610 in large letters. Shoving the wallet and key into a pocket of her black cargos, taking care to button down the flap, Modeen looked over at the house again.

Still no movement.

Turning back to the carnage around her, the battered Hyundai and the body in the gutter, she strode to the rear of the Toyota.

Seeing an aluminium toolbox bolted to its flat tray back, she opened it. Inside was a neatly coiled tow rope. She took out the rope and placed it on the tray, and then went around to climb back into the driver's seat and move the ute into position in front of the Hyundai.

Grabbing the night vision goggles from out of her duffel which was still in the hire car, she resumed her search for the gun. As she stepped into the gutter, scanning left to right, she stumbled over what she thought was a small log. But looking down she realised it was a boot, still attached to the lower part of a leg now a mangled mess of shattered bone and torn flesh.

Shuddering and stepping back, she glanced at the body some fifteen metres away.

*The leg must've been torn off by the blast and blown over the top of the Toyota.*

She sat on her haunches to stare thoughtfully at the severed limb. After a few moments she rose and, gritting her teeth, gingerly scooped it up. Turning her head away from the gruesome object in her arms, she hurried to the Hyundai where she lay the torn limb on the driver's side floor. Then she went over to where the corpse was slowly stiffening in the gutter. She put her hands under the arms and heaved the dead weight out and onto the road. From there she proceeded to drag it to the hire car. A booted foot on one side of the body trailed behind in the dirt, while the ragged stump on the other side left a damp crimson trail in the dust.

With a grunt, Modeen dumped Mazlin's inert remains into the front seat and slipped the seatbelt over a drooping shoulder. Then she straightened and wiped her hands on her pants. Reaching in to turn the key in the ignition, she was relieved when the Hyundai's motor coughed into life.

She put her foot on the brake and shifted the auto lever into neutral before stepping back to close the door. Remembering her duffel, she reached in through the driver's window past the glassy-eyed corpse, and grabbed the bag from the passenger seat.

As she pulled the unzipped duffel through the window it twisted and gaped open, and her binoculars fell out. They tumbled down her leg and slid under the car.

With a frustrated exhalation, Modeen got down on her knees and felt around under the vehicle. When her searching fingers brushed over something metal, she gave a satisfied nod … and then frowned. Pausing, she felt around the metal item and traced fingertips down something smooth, square and barrel-like. With a pleased grin, she grasped the item and pulled it out from beneath the car.

Sitting back, she gazed down at the jet black Glock in her hand.

*Well hello there.*

She turned it over, checking for damage but there was none visible. Tucking the weapon into the waistband of her pants, she collected her binoculars and jogged over to the Toyota. After tethering the Hyundai to it with the tow rope, she jumped into the driver's seat, shoved the ute into 4WD and first gear, and pulled the idling hire car out of the gutter. Then, with the Hyundai in tow, she headed toward the homestead.

The gravel road passed through a rusted-open farm gate and then diminished until all that remained of it were two worn tyre tracks.

The Toyota's headlights illuminated the area in front of her but Modeen wanted more.

Feeling around under the dash she found a toggle switch and flicked it on. Immediately two CB Super Oscar spotlights mounted on the roll bar at the rear of the ute's cab burst into life. Their powerful beams lit up the homestead as if it were a stage set at the Sydney Opera House. But apart from startling a mob of kangaroos in the front paddock, some of whom bounced away, everything remained quiet.

Closer in, it was clear the homestead was in dire need of repair. The wide verandas jutting out from three sides of the building were on a lean, and their timber flooring was gapped, uneven, or missing altogether.

The roof guttering was broken and hanging off in places, and the once red corrugated iron roofing was faded and rusted, its dominant colour now a vague brown.

To the side of the house a chook run lay empty, its wire netting sagging and torn, and beside it a tractor was just visible beneath clumps of tall grass and weeds.

As Modeen got closer, she glimpsed two large gas cylinders also sitting amid knee-high grass at the left side of the house, against the outer wall of what she guessed to be the kitchen. Pulling up twenty metres from the house, she took out the Glock and dropped the clip from its base.

Six rounds remained.

Palming the clip back into place, she stepped from the vehicle and made her way to the house. As she crept up the stairs the creak and groan of old, distressed timbers was the only sound to be heard. A worn-thin welcome mat greeted her at the base of the front door, and beside it sat a bristled boot scraper. Made from cast iron and shaped like an elephant beetle, it was festooned with cobwebs, and the last boot mud it had removed had turned to dust long ago. Mounted at head height along the aged weatherboards on either side of the front door, metal hooks that would have held many a stockman's hat and oilskin coat in years gone by, now hung crumbling and useless from rusting nails.

Keeping her ears tuned for any sound, Modeen turned the ancient brass handle and was surprised when the front door opened a crack. Leaning back against the door jamb, she palmed the solid old door open the rest of the way. It groaned and squealed on dry hinges that strained under the weight.

Holding the pistol in front of her, she stepped inside, where a stale, damp smell greeted her. Above her head a bare light bulb hung from the ceiling, its pale light casting a dismal glow over the immediate surroundings. When a small red LED attached to a security camera in the far corner of the room caught her eye, she didn't hesitate. Raising the Glock, she fired off a round. As the camera burst apart its main housing whacked against the tongue and grove wall and split open, to dangle pathetically from a single wire.

The back of her neck tingled. Something wasn't right. Thinking *this is a setup*, she backed out of the house again and retreated to the Toyota, scanning to left, right and behind as she went. Staring back at the house for what seemed like a long minute, she was curious when nothing happened. She climbed into the ute and nosed it forward, lining it up with the gas bottles beside the house.

Once in place, she backed up to release the slack on the tow rope, and then disconnected it before moving the Toyota a distance away.

Going back to the Hyundai, she leaned through the

window and tried to shift it into drive, but the lever wouldn't budge. She rolled her eyes.

*Damn! They build too many safeguards into these new cars.*

Opening the door, she realised she'd need something to prop against the accelerator. The obvious implement lay on the floor, but she grimaced at the thought of touching it again. When nothing else presented itself, she had to swallow her revulsion. Forcing herself to once more scoop up the severed leg, she pushed the boot against the accelerator and wedged the other end of the limb against the base of the seat. The hire car's motor revved at the pressure on the accelerator.

Opening the driver's door as wide as it would go, she used her own foot to press down on the brake. Bracing herself, she reached in to shift the gear lever into Drive and then threw herself back. As the vehicle jolted forward she turned and loped away, glancing over her shoulder every few steps to make sure the doomed Hyundai continued hurtling toward its target.

It struck the gas cylinders with a sharp bang, ramming them into and through the walls of the old homestead, and then disappeared from sight as the house collapsed around it. Seconds later an ear-splitting explosion sent Modeen ducking for cover beside the Toyota, as wooden splinters and sheets of rusted roofing iron rained down around her.

*No way those gas cylinders could've created an explosion of that magnitude on their own.*

The flames from the blazing homestead glowed brilliant red in the Toyota's rear view mirrors as Modeen drove out the gate of Reger's farm. She stopped at Johnston Road and consulted her maps app again, before turning left and continuing south toward the Forest Highway from where it was a forty-five minute drive to Bunbury. A light flashing from the ute's centre console caught her attention and she glanced down to see a mobile phone vibrating there – Mazlin's no doubt. It displayed a caller ID of 'JR' on the screen.

Returning her gaze to the road, she let the call ring out.

At the Australind turn-off, she slowed as blue and red flashing lights appeared on the horizon and the shriek of sirens reached her ears. An ambulance, fire truck, and other support vehicles sped past, heading in the opposite direction. Changing down a gear, Modeen accelerated and the Toyota's turbo engine responded eagerly.

She rolled down the window to let in some fresh air, and clear away any lingering smell of smoke in the cab, and motored into Bunbury.

# CHAPTER TWENTY

Cruising down Blair Street, Modeen headed toward the Leschenault Inlet and Bunbury's city centre. At twenty-three hundred hours the flow of traffic had reduced to a dribble at best, and finding a car park was easy. Turning left at a roundabout onto Symmons Street, she pulled into the deserted parking lot behind a Rivers Super Store and nosed the Toyota in close against the building.

Killing the engine, she made sure no one was around before taking a moment to once more check the Glock.

Five bullets left in the clip.

She got out, stretched and took a deep breath. Then, moving with a heightened air of purpose, she opened the ute's back door and reached into her duffel to take out a white T-shirt and black woollen balaclava. Wrapping the gun in the balaclava, she tucked it firmly into the waistband of her pants before pulling on the white shirt over the black one she was already wearing. After checking the hotel room key was still in the pocket of her black cargos, she locked the Toyota and set off for the easy walk to the Lord Forest Hotel.

As she strode out of the carpark and around the corner, her eyes were drawn to the Bunbury Tower building. Dubbed the Milk Carton by locals because of its funky, wedge-shaped roof and white colouring, it rose to dominate the skyline and dwarf the more sedate Lord Forrest Hotel alongside it.

Sauntering past the tower, where only one or two lights burned from the offices within, Modeen skipped up a short flight of steps and into the Lord Forrest's expansive, glassed entrance. She paused there for a quick scan of the building's interior.

A central atrium on the ground floor housed the hotel's reception area, indoor wading pool, restaurant, bar and function rooms. Landscaped limestone borders created winding pathways around the pool, while strategically placed palm trees and broad-leafed plants gave the area a pleasant, sub-tropical feel. Rising from the atrium to completely encircle it were multiple floors of apartments, of varying sizes and levels of luxury. The planting boxes built into the solid white balustrading on each floor dripped with greenery, lush vines and fronds that cascaded downward as though stretching leafy, covetous fingers for the earth.

From the function room to the right of the bar came

muffled laughter and cheering as what sounded like a wedding moved into the toasts and speeches stage of proceedings. At an eruption of laughter from the bar, Modeen glanced over to see a group of well-dressed patrons watching the proficient barman, wearing a dark blue battle jacket, matching pants and cummerbund, mix, pour and serve with aplomb a variety of cocktails.

As he placed the latest concoction in front of a woman seated somewhat unsteadily on a bar stool, he lit the sparkler in the glass and it burst into a brilliant shower of sparks. This met with awed gasps and applause, and even from where she was standing Modeen could hear calls of, 'Yeah! I'll have one of them too!'

Turning to eye the area to the left of the atrium where the stairwell and lift were located, she decided she needed to stretch her muscles and get her circulation pumping. She made her way to the door of the stairwell and opened it. Hesitating, she checked behind to see if anyone was lurking or watching.

No one was.

Going through the doorway, she climbed the stairs to the first level and read the room numbers displayed in shiny brass on the wall near the landing. She repeated the process until she'd reached the right level. Moving quietly along the wide walkway, she noted the number on the first door she came to.

Room 608.

Returning soundlessly to the stairwell she slipped back down to the landing below and then paused to listen. When she heard nothing but the sounds of merrymaking coming from the atrium, she peeled off the white T-shirt, leaving on the black one beneath it. She dropped the white shirt in the stairwell.

Plucking the pistol from under her waistband, she unwrapped it from the balaclava which she proceeded to don, covering her platinum blonde head and completing her all-black shroud.

Pulling back and releasing the slide on the Glock, she took a deep breath and sprinted back up the stairs, extracting the room key from her pocket on the fly.

She didn't pause on reaching the floor, where she strode past doors 608 and 609 with the barest of glances at them.

At room 610, she stopped.

Thrusting the key into the slot, she raised the gun and shoved the door open. Inside the room, Jon Reger sat at a desk with a laptop in front of him. He didn't bother turning at the sound of the door, merely barked over his shoulder, 'It's about time, Leila.'

Modeen stepped inside and snarled, 'Guess again,' raising the Glock as she spoke.

An instant later the pistol was knocked from her hand as the door slammed into her. Thrown off balance, she staggered sideways as a man holding a Barretta appeared from behind the door. Throwing her an evil sneer he planted his feet, straightened his arm and took aim at her head.

Too slow.

Just as his finger curled against the trigger, she darted forward and deflected the gun with a sharp blow from her right hand. The shot rang out and the bullet lodged in the nearby wall. Rising to her toes, she spun anti-clockwise toward the man, using the momentum and all her weight to drive her left elbow into the centre of his solar plexus. The force of the blow winded him and sent him backward, doubled over. She moved with him to lace both hands behind his head and force it lower. With a swivel of her hips to create impetus, she brought up her knee and cracked his head against it.

As he fell backward unconscious, Modeen heard a roar and whipped around to see Reger's charging six foot three frame spring at her in a rugby-style tackle. He had four inches and about a hundred kilos on her, there was no way she could avoid or deflect the assault.

When he barrelled into her and threw her backward, she grabbed the front of his shirt and brought up her knees. As her back hit the floor, she rolled and used the power of her legs and his momentum to execute a Judo *tomoe nage* circular throw, tossing him over the top of her and catapulting him though the door. He landed heavily on his back and skidded into the concrete balustrade.

Before he could get to his feet, Modeen was on him. She followed through with what Spooky often described as her 'classic soccer kick' to the head. While managing to lift a beefy arm to deflect some of the blow's force, Reger was clearly rattled. He staggered to his feet, wiping away blood from the corner of his mouth with the back of a hand. Seeing the blood, he swore loudly and threw her a filthy look. Clenching his fists, he bunched up to resume the attack, and that's when she saw her opening.

She sprang lithely onto the balls of her feet and moved toward him, turning a full three hundred and sixty degrees to execute a powerful spinning back kick. She slammed her jackbooted heel against his temple and then spun to a crouching stop to watch his eyes roll back and his head sag sideways. His body remained rigid but the impact of the blow had driven him onto his toes and twisted him sideways against the balustrade. For a brief moment he teetered there, mouth agape, and then, as though in slow motion, he tumbled over the top.

Not waiting to hear the gruesome sound of the heavy body falling from height onto an unyielding surface, Modeen darted back into the apartment. She went straight to the open laptop, a Macbook Pro with a small storage device protruding from the side USB port. Running her fingers over the built-in mouse pad, she was checking the on-board hard disk for files when a dark face filled the screen in front of her.

The man stared at her for a second and then his eyes narrowed. 'Who are you?' he snarled, 'and where's Reger?' Tribal tattoos covered one whole side of his face, and when he spoke she glimpsed the inside of his lips and mouth.

They were stained black.

Replying coolly, 'Reger's dead,' Modeen moved her fingers surreptitiously over the keyboard to take a screen dump of his image. 'It's over.'

'Hah!' His matted dreadlocks danced as his head rocked back. '*One* man is dead and you think it's *over?*' Straightening to glare at her once more, his lips twisted. 'I have a hundred just like him.'

'A hundred, is that right?' Dragging the screen dump to the USB storage device, she ground out through clenched teeth, 'Well, when I'm through, you're going to need more.'

His sneer vanished and his voice grew coldly calculating. 'What is it you want?' Leaning closer to the screen at his end, he peered at her. 'And who are you? Show me your face.'

Her only response was to yank out the memory stick and slam the laptop closed. Hearing shouts and cries from below, she sprinted from the room. At the stairwell she tugged off the balaclava and hurriedly donned the white T-shirt again before racing down the stairs.

When two male staff members met her in the stairwell on level four, she yelled, 'Level six, hurry!' and pointed upward.

The men nodded their thanks and resumed their rushed climb. She watched them taking the steps two at a time and then continued down the stairs to the ground floor. Coming out of the stairwell door, she flicked a glance at the group of shocked onlookers gathered around Reger's broken, inert body.

Appalled gasps and hushed murmurs of, 'He's dead,' and, 'Of course he's dead, he fell from way up there,' reached her ears as she skirted around the ghoulish throng to make her way to the front door.

Once outside, she paused on the footpath to breathe in the fresh air before crossing the street. As she headed to where she'd left the Toyota, the familiar sound of approaching sirens assaulted her ears.

Moments later a police car flew around the corner headed toward the Lord Forrest, red and blue lights strobing harshly in the dimness.

Slipping around the back of the Rivers store, she unlocked the ute and climbed inside. Placing both hands on the steering wheel she rested her forehead on them, closed her eyes, and took a few deep, calming breaths. Knowing it wasn't safe to linger – or be found anywhere in the vicinity for that matter – she opened an internet page on her phone and quickly checked for available flights from Perth to Brisbane. Scrolling through the options, she found a Virgin flight departing at o-five thirty the next day that would have her in Brisbane early that afternoon. Thankful it would give her plenty of time for the drive back to Perth, she booked a seat.

At o-three hundred hours, Perth's domestic airport was brightly lit against the night sky but the roads in and out of it were free of the usual daytime traffic snarls. Even the number of waiting taxis had dwindled to just a few, and their drivers were taking advantage of the quiet to catch a few winks.

Driving into the short-term parking area, Modeen chose a bay in a dimly-lit corner and parked Mazlin's Toyota for the last time.

Taking care to wipe the ute clean of any remaining fingerprints, she grabbed her duffel from the back seat. Purposely leaving the keys dangling in the ignition and the driver's window down, she set off for the Virgin terminal without looking back.

After passing through security, she bought a coffee and sipped it as she strode to the departure lounge, flicking the empty cup into a bin along the way. Sinking gratefully into a chair in a quiet corner, she put her head back and closed her eyes.

# CHAPTER TWENTY-ONE

Modeen was one of the first to board the Virgin Airbus A380 for the flight to Brisbane. She'd booked a window seat this time in the hope of catching some sleep over the six and a half hour flight. After taking her seat she studied the other passengers as they shuffled past along the corridor, glancing anxiously at the row and seat numbers as they went.

Young, old, fat, slim, accompanied, alone, calm, nervous … the passing parade had a bit of everything except, thankfully, sharp eyes staring interrogatively back at her.

As the line of passengers thinned and the flight attendants began their pre-flight spiels, Modeen turned to gaze out the window. The night's gloom lingered over the tarmac and buildings, but the morning sky was slowly brightening in the east with the promise of a clear day.

'Ladies and gentlemen, welcome aboard flight VA465 to Brisbane.' The flight attendant's voice was broadcast through the speakers. 'The captain has turned on the Fasten Seatbelts sign. If you haven't already done so, please stow your carry-on luggage under the seat in front of you or in one of the overhead lockers, take your seat and ensure your seatbelts are fastened.'

Leaning forward to free the ends of her seatbelt and fasten it low over her hips, Modeen felt the chain around her neck shift as the ring dangling from it rolled over the sensitive skin of her breast bone. Pulling it out from beneath her shirt, her eyes softened as she gazed at the ring, turning it over and over in her fingers.

So engrossed was she in her thoughts, she barely noticed the slow-moving, grey-haired man take the aisle seat one across from her in the row.

After settling himself, he looked over and watched her for a while before saying kindly, 'I gave my wife a ring similar to that.'

His old, raspy voice broke her out of her reverie. Seeing her hastily tuck the ring back under her shirt, he gave a rueful smile. 'Sorry if I disturbed you.'

'It's alright. I was just….' The lump in her throat made it hard to speak, so she finished the sentence by exhaling and throwing him a tense smile.

'I know. Thinking of someone special, and if I'm right, the man who gave you that ring.' At her tight-lipped nod in reply, he regarded her levelly. 'You flying home to him?'

She gave another slow nod as the plane began taxiing down the runway.

'Well,' the man said with a ring of finality in his voice, 'he's one lucky bloke.' Facing the front again he tucked a travel pillow behind his neck, put his head back, and closed his eyes.

Modeen regarded him for another moment before turning to stare out the window at the grey blur of the tarmac below the accelerating plane. As the ground fell away from beneath the jet's wings, she sighed and rested her head against the window.

Closing her eyes, she finally unleashed the thoughts she'd resolutely pushed to the back of her mind over the past few days and they flooded in. Thoughts of Wolf ... their first meeting as raw army recruits, the years of service together, the challenge and reward of getting to know the man beneath the tough soldier exterior, their growing intimate bond.

And finally, her thoughts turned to what the future might hold for them.

She spent the whole flight engrossed in her thoughts, sometimes smiling, often swallowing and brushing away tears, and the time passed quickly. It seemed more like minutes than hours later she was collecting her duffel from the baggage carousel at Brisbane domestic airport.

After making her way to the long term parking, she

collected her GTR, strapped her duffel to the bike and donned her helmet. Climbing aboard, she started the motor and nosed the big bike out of the parking bay. As she accelerated away she let the rushing wind blow over her as though to clear her mind and refresh her body, before leaning low over the tank to speed straight to the hospital.

It was sixteen hundred hours when she entered the ICU. Finding Wolf lying exactly as she had left him three days before, she felt like they were in some sort of time warp, one she wished they could escape and find themselves back before....

Shaking her head to clear it of ridiculous fancies, she bent over him to drop a kiss on his forehead.

He smelled of Sapaderm soap and man – a familiar, cherished man – and she breathed him in before taking a seat on the edge of his bed.

Taking his hand in hers she gazed hopefully into his face. 'Hey Troy, I'm back.'

The large, strong hand between hers lay still, the skin cool, and his face remained closed, immobile, expressionless. But as she stared at him she could sense life under the stillness, a fire idling beneath the surface.

Or was that just wishful thinking?

*Keep it real, that's what he'd want.*

She swallowed and squeezed his hand. 'I got him, Troy. I got the b—'

Biting back the bilious fury rising within her, she made herself say calmly, 'Reger got what he deserved.' Gazing at his impassive face, she leaned closer to tenderly brush the dark hair back from his forehead. Lowering her voice, she began relating all that had happened since she last saw him. She was still talking to him when two nurses bustled into the room an hour later.

'Changing the linen,' one of them announced imperiously as they ushered her out and drew the curtains around his bed. 'Come back in half an hour.'

She wandered down the corridor to the common room and headed straight to the coffee machine. Taking out a two dollar coin, she inserted it in the slot and placed a styrofoam cup under the nozzle, as a familiar voice said behind her, 'I'll have a flat white, one sugar, thanks.'

Turning, she saw Ben sitting in the corner, mobile phone in his hand. He stared at her without smiling.

'Hey Ben. Sorry, didn't know you were here.'

He narrowed his eyes at her. 'I could say the same to you.'

Turning back to the machine, she inserted another coin and waited for the coffees. He didn't speak again, and the silence hung thick in the air. There was a grilling coming, of that she was intuitively certain. Taking a deep breath, she grabbed both cups and went over to sit beside him, passing him a coffee. He didn't even take a sip before putting the cup on the table in front of them, spilling some of its contents in the process.

Uncaring, he held up his NatSec phone so that she could clearly see the display and barked, 'Who's this?'

Looking at the screen from over the rim of her cup, Modeen saw a green dot with a small TD9315 tag above it. By its surroundings, she estimated its location to be somewhere in inner Sydney.

*Aunty Hann must've gone home, taking my NatSec tracking device with her.*

Seeing her lips compress as she lowered her eyes to stare into her coffee, Ben said crisply, 'For the last few days, whoever TD9315 is,' and he waved the phone at her, 'has been going to and from the Gold Coast convention centre and your Surfers Paradise apartment.'

Pulling back the phone, he tapped the display and bought up a YouTube clip. After hitting PLAY he once more held up the phone so she could see the screen. She watched the grainy image of a dark, balaclava wearing figure executing a spinning back kick, striking a heavily built man. When he tumbled over a nearby balustrade, the person holding the camera could be heard giving a shocked cry, and the footage shook violently before coming to a blurry end.

Modeen blinked hard. Surmising from the camera angle that someone on the same level but the other side of the hotel must have heard the gun shot and captured the fight on a phone, she said defensively, 'That could be anyone.'

Ben raised a sceptical eyebrow. 'There aren't many female left footers out there trained to that level.' When she didn't speak, he leaned forward to eye her. 'I've stuck my neck out for you, JD. For one thing, I had to do some fast talking to the hire car company and the WA police when your hire car was found, not to mention Jack. They took some convincing that the vehicle was stolen, and that it wasn't your burnt corpse in the driver's seat … something I only knew because I was monitoring your credit card transactions.'

'The car was insured,' she muttered under her breath without meeting his eyes.

He shook his head. 'If you were so determined to go after Reger, why didn't you tell me? I could've endorsed the mission as a NatSec operation and provided you with safeguards and resources. And how did you know where to find him, anyway?'

She threw him a chagrined look but didn't answer.

'We'll discuss that later. For now, I want to reiterate that going off the radar like you did meant you were on your own. If they'd known what you were doing, Bugs and Spook would've insisted on going along.'

'That's exactly why I did this alone.' She met his eyes with a tearful gaze. 'This was something I *had* to do, and I was afraid NatSec wouldn't approve my involvement, considering….' She sniffed and swallowed before going on. 'Look what happened to Wolf. I couldn't bear it if the same thing or worse happened to any of you … because of me. This was *my* vendetta, and I was prepared to risk no one but myself.'

He put a hand on her shoulder. 'With all we've been through over the years, you should've had more faith in us, JD, and given us the opportunity to help you. I might be hamstrung by protocols, but that doesn't mean I can't work the system when necessary.' His voice softened. 'We're agents, JD, we all understand the risks that come with the choices we make.'

'Yes, and this was *my* choice, not my team's.'

Sighing, he sat back to regard her for a long moment before speaking again. 'NatSec wanted Reger neutralised, that's our saving grace.'

'Don't you mean *my* saving grace?'

'We're all in this together, JD. That's what team-work is all about.'

She nodded and bowed her head.

'We survived active military service because we were a close knit team. We respected each other as highly trained soldiers, and we watched each other's backs.' Ben paused before saying calmly, 'Will you promise me that this is over, that you won't go disappearing again?'

She locked eyes with him and said quietly, 'I quit Ben. I don't want to do this anymore.'

He frowned and shook his head, but before he could speak she said, 'It's what Wolf wanted.' Swallowing the lump in her throat, she went on in a strangled voice, 'As I told you before, he wanted us to leave and try to start a normal life … together.'

Ben exhaled and his broad shoulders drooped. Leaning forward, he rested his elbows on his knees and said slowly, 'Look, JD, I'd never try to force you or any of my team members to stay if you want out, I wouldn't want that on my conscience. That decision has to be yours. But I want you to remember that there are other positions you could hold in the organisation, ones that don't carry the same level of risk.'

She frowned. 'Like what?'

'Well, with your self defence skills, I'm sure I could talk Jack into making you a trainer.' Ben took a sip of coffee and watched her, hoping for a positive response.

When her expression remained stubbornly determined, he sighed. 'Just take at least a week to think it over, JD. Then, if you still want out, I'll go ahead and submit the paperwork.' Draining his cup, he glanced at his watch and rose to his feet. 'I have to head back to Melbourne.' He looked down the corridor toward Wolf's room. 'The doctors aren't expecting any change in his condition, at least for a while. But they know to contact me immediately if there *is* any change. And the same goes for you.'

Modeen had risen with him, and moved in to hug him goodbye. 'Thanks Ben, your support means a lot to me.'

He wrapped his arms tightly around her and then abruptly let her go. With a final parting nod, he strode away, leaving her staring after him, deep in thought.

A short while later she walked back into Wolf's room to find him once more alone and motionless on a freshly made bed. Leaning over him, she kissed his forehead and then squeezed his hand, whispering, 'I've had a big day, Troy. I'll be back to see you tomorrow.'

In the waning heat of the day, Modeen found the ride back to Surfers Paradise soothing. It felt good to be doing something, to be moving, and she enjoyed the sensation of freedom she got from riding her GTR. Even so, she was feeling the lack of sleep, and was relieved she'd have the apartment to herself again.

When she let herself in, she found the thank you card and gift basket her aunt had left on the kitchen counter. Smiling fondly, she went into her bedroom and dumped her duffel in the corner. Peeling off her clothes, she headed straight to the ensuite for a long shower. Dressing in a cotton singlet and shorts, she flopped onto the bed, stretching her arms above her head and closing her eyes. She was just drifting off to sleep when she suddenly remembered the USB memory stick ... Reger's.

Jumping up, she pulled her cargo pants out of the laundry hamper and dug around in the pocket until her searching fingers brushed over the stick. She took it out and grabbed her laptop, before sitting on the bed again and plugging the memory stick into her computer's USB port.

It opened the sixteen gigabit device straightaway, and she leaned closer to peer at what the stick contained. It turned out to be just a few Word documents and a couple of Excel spreadsheets. Sifting through the files, she perused a profit and loss statement and was about to close the file when she noticed ten names listed in a table beneath the main one.

Reger's name was third on the list.

Modeen grew still, and then breathed out deeply and closed her eyes.

*One down, nine to go.*

# # #

*If you've enjoyed MODEEN CONVERGENCE I hope you'll consider posting a review on your retailer's site.*
*FHJ*

# PRAISE FOR FRANK H JORDAN

'Holy Butt Kickers Batman! Frank Jordan can write a wicked story that mixes humor, adventure, and intrigue woven into a realistic plot. His characters are gritty and tough as nails. Love the accents and the people of Oz.'

— US REVIEWER

… [Jordan has] created a match for the baddies in Jo Modeen, a kick-ass heroine with nerves of steel and a size 9 boot….'

— THE CAIRNS POST NEWSPAPER

'There ain't nuthin' [sic] to dislike about Jo Modeen. Would love to [have] had her on our team back in Cambodia and Laos!'

— REVIEWER JR LEE

# THE MODEEN FACTOR

*Introducing kick-butt heroine Jo Modeen*
*She's beautiful, noble … and deadly*

Josephine Dakota Modeen, recipient of the Medal for Gallantry in Action and the first woman to be accepted into the elite SASR, finds life after the Army unfulfilling. When contacted by her old CO, she knows it's not a social call. Ben Logan VC MG doesn't 'do' social calls, at least not to the members of his old squad now living in the 'real' world. Hearing from Ben means a mission, no exceptions….

*The books in this series are available in ebook, paperback, and in ebook box sets of three. The first three instalments are also available as audio books from selected retailers.*

# THE MODEEN TRANSFORMATION

*The 2nd action-filled Modeen adventure*

Australian security agencies are on alert in the lead-up
to the 2014 international G20 Summit being held in
Brisbane, Queensland. Although aware of an increase
in web activity on the summit site and into the
backgrounds of its attending diplomats, even NatSec
intel can't know what the terrorist group known as
'The Spear of Allah' is planning.
Something ex-SASR soldier and now NatSec agent, Jo
Modeen, is about to find out in a very personal way....

# MODEEN ROGUE

*The 5th Modeen high-octane thriller*

Decorated ex-special forces soldier and now national
security agent Josephine Dakota Modeen struggles to
come to terms with the fate of close teammate Troy
'Wolf' Wolverton. Critically injured during the team's
most recent mission, he lies comatose in Brisbane
Hospital's intensive care unit.
And the prognosis for his recovery isn't good.
Driven to pursue the organisation responsible, Modeen
embarks on an unauthorised campaign of retribution.
A campaign that is both personal and perilous.

# MODEEN REDEMPTION

*The 6th Modeen adventure*

In a high-tech Australian laboratory, final testing is underway of a deadly new prototype, a weapon that could alter the course of modern warfare and cement America's position as the world's dominant superpower.
The US Department of Defence is understandably anxious about security at the laboratory and tasks NatSec with providing additional on-ground surveillance.
No matter the cost, the prototype cannot be allowed to fall into the wrong hands....

# MODEEN: FLASHPOINT

*The 8th explosive adventure*

When an LNG tanker is sunk in the Philippine Sea north of Papua New Guinea, the spotlight falls on the lucrative liquefied natural gas market. Believing an international cartel to be responsible, and that Australia's LNG plants could be at risk, the CIA tasks NatSec with gathering on-site intel.

Modeen's team is deployed to discover the saboteurs' identities, determine their next target, and find out just how far they will go....

# THE JO MODEEN BOX SET: BOOKS 1-3

Book one *The Modeen Factor*, introduces decorated
Australian Special Forces soldier Josephine Modeen,
the kick-ass heroine we'd all like to have on our side.
After leaving the military, Modeen is recruited by her
old CO, now a team leader with national security
agency NatSec.

Book two *The Modeen Transformation*, and book three
*Modeen Black Ops*, take us along on car chases, hostage
rescues, and battles with terrorists, where Modeen's
mantra is always the same … go hard or go home.

Available as an ebook from your favourite online
retailer.

# THE JO MODEEN BOX SET: BOOKS 4-6

In *Modeen Convergence,* Modeen's team converges in far north Queensland on what becomes a complex mission with dangerous links to the past.

In *Modeen Rogue,* our heroine embarks on an unauthorised campaign of retribution. She's going rogue … and going alone.

In *Modeen Redemption,* NatSec is tasked with keeping safe the DOD's latest and most advanced weapon. A weapon that could alter the course of modern warfare. And must be kept secure at all costs….

The second box set is available as an ebook from your favourite online retailer.